GOOD KARMA

A Dog's Life

A Novel

Matthew Calloway

ISBN: 9798866866687

DEDICATION

For Karma
&
My Family

A NOTE TO THE READER

What follows is based on the life of a real dog. Her tale is impossible to tell without the human characters she encountered, and that is where our story crosses into the realm of fiction.

I have done my best to present a readable and entertaining work, but it will no doubt fall short of doing Karma justice. There were no editors, agents, or publishers involved, just your humble author and his laptop. All I would ask of you, dear reader, is that whatever shortcomings you may find in my telling of her tale, please don't think poorly of Karma for them. She was truly good.

Chapter One

When I was nineteen, I thought the whole world was waiting for me. I had a promising career and a nice apartment. I was with my first love and every part of my life was full of hope.

And then… I was 25. Racking up debts, crashing at my brother's house, working at the same video store I worked at when I was sixteen, and bawling my eyes out on my grandmother's shoulder after hearing that my first love, Katherine, was going to marry someone else.

I was sad and angry and ashamed. My brother Peter and my cousin Ben talked to my neighbor Tom; they decided that I needed help. Peter reached out to Jude, my oldest friend, and together they all arranged a huge party to try and cheer me up.

Our place was dirty and free. There was a standing cloud of smoke in those late winter months, thick with the odor of kerosene, and almost every night was a party. The guys had decided my condition called for something special, something that would live on for years in rumors and memories.

They made a bonfire from the scraps of the halfpipe we had built; people were flying around on skateboards and bikes while my brother's band was playing up on the deck of the ramp. Girls were singing, guys were fighting; it really was epic. Ben and Tom had brought their Pit-bulls and I mostly just lingered outside the firelight with the dogs, watching other people enjoy their lives.

I never wanted a dog. Ben tried to push pups on everyone when they confirmed his girl was going to have a litter. My Nana had adopted a sweet Pit-mix named Grace from Peter when he worked at a rescue shelter, and my old roommate Robert had a husky that was cool, but dog parenting just didn't seem like something I wanted or needed. Jude and his girlfriend Mary had adopted two dogs, a Spaniel and a Chihuahua-mix, when they moved in together. Jude was adamant that I had to get one.

"You need a dog Mark, seriously!"

"Seriously, I can barely take care of myself. Why do I wanna add another responsibility to this mix?"

"It'll never be right if you don't get a dog, trust me dude."

"What won't be right?"

"The universe! You're going to have to love something new eventually, it might as well be a puppy!"

He and I were high school friends, snowboarding buddies, and road trip companions in the early days after graduation. We once showed up to work three hours late after driving all night back from Mardi Gras. My boss was furious and told me to go fix a computer in the training room while he decided if I still had a job. I walked into a classroom of new hires and that's when I met and fell in love with Katherine. She introduced Jude and I to Mary and our first double date was set.

The four of us did everything together until I moved to the city, then our group slowly drifted apart until Kat and I eventually split up. I ghosted almost everyone I knew after that and moved to California to try and start over. I wasn't out west a whole year before I found myself on a Greyhound bus back to Tennessee with my head down and my tail tucked. The dogs had already taken my place as Jude and Mary's best friends by then and, shamefully, I think I resented all dogs for that.

Seven weeks passed; Jude constantly assuring me that the universe demanded that I had to get one of those puppies.

On the morning of my 26th birthday, I went to see my grandmother. She had been a widow for two years and lived alone with Grace. She missed Grandpap, but never complained about being lonely. She always said she was just thankful for all the memories and experiences they'd shared, and for the family they'd built together. Most often you'd find her on the back porch reminiscing with a smile while Grace played in the yard. That day was no different and she met me in the driveway with a big hug.

"Happy Birthday to my Sweetpea!"

"Thank you, thank you! How's my Nana today?"

"Oh, me and Gracie are gettin' along fine! I was tellin' her, I thought we might get a visitor today."

Nana's place was surrounded by acres and acres of crop fields. Some years it was corn reaching for the stars, others it was wheat swaying in the wind. That year it was soybeans, and they mostly just sat there being green until Grace came charging out of them and across the yard to greet me with dirty paws and a few licks of my hand. I repaid her with a little pat on the head.

"You keepin' Nana straight Gracie?"

She answered with a bark and a few wags of her tail.

Nana smiled, "Ben tells me you're gettin' a pup soon…"

"Nana, I think Ben's just tryin' to recruit you into helping him find homes for them all!"

"Maybe so, but I think you should… Dogs have a way with broken hearts."

"I made some bad choices Nana, and karma came back

around to bite me. I'm not so sure gettin' something else to bite me is the best idea. Besides, there's a new cat in my life now, did you hear about our stray?"

"Lizzie said something about a kitten wandering up that had lost its tail?!"

"No, no, that's just the breed, they're called Manx. She looks like a little bobcat. Pete was carrying the trash out and this skunk comes out of nowhere at him. He froze in the driveway and the skunk started rearing up at him, then this cat flies across the yard and starts attacking the skunk. He said it sounded like a Kung-Fu movie."

"King who?"

"Kung-Fu. You know, those movies where everyone is jumpin' around shouting and kickin' each other in the face? Anyways, the cat chased the skunk off and followed Pete inside, then she just hopped on the couch like she was supposed to be there."

"Well Lawd! I'll have to come see her one of these days, but I still think a dog would do you good. They can teach us an awful lot."

Before we got into a debate about what a dog could possibly teach a human, I told her I had to be moving on to my next stop. She gave me a big hug and a kiss on my cheek, then she waved goodbye in the rearview my whole way down her driveway and yelled,

"Thanks for the visit baby, I love my Sweetpea!"

I caught school traffic at the road. Yellow buses went by like boxcars, filled with kids counting down the few remaining days to summer break. I turned around to see Nana playing with Grace while I waited. They looked so happy together that I felt a tinge of envy. I figured Nana was almost always right, maybe a furry friend would do me good. With the end of that bus line nowhere in sight, I called up Ben.

"I'll take your meanest boy."

"They're pure Pit, Cuz, I'm sure they'll all be mean!"

"Well, I'll take your biggest then!"

"Me and Tom ain't keepin' none, you can have pick of the litter. Should be a couple-three weeks 'for she pops, then we'll have to ween 'em for about six more."

"Just let me know. Hey, you comin' to the party tonight?"

"Nah, I gotta be out early tomorrow to take care of some things but hey, happy birthday Cuz!"

"Thank you, sir! You'll be missed!"

The train of buses passed and I decided to get my quarterly visit with my parents out of the way. They had separated right after Peter graduated then, after a few years apart, had reconciled and were living in Nana's mother's old place a few miles away.

Nana and Grandpap had bought the place to keep Nana's mom close in her final years, then my mom had taken it over after my folks split. When they got back together, my dad had this feeling the value of houses would be going down and decided to sell his place to move in with her.

Liz and Dan, as I called my folks back then, both came out to meet me in the yard.

"Happy Birthday!!! How's my firstborn on his 26th birthday?" Mom asked with glee.

"Looking forward to tonight, how are Liz and Dan?"

She hated it when I called them by their names. Dad took his turn at the plate while she recovered from the blow.

"We're glad to have you close to home again Son, happy birthday! Are you getting out tonight?"

"Just another night at home. Jude and Mary may stop by,

but I'm prob'ly just skating and playing music with the guys."

Mom chimed in, with her sharpest mother tone,

"…and drinking?"

I didn't even acknowledge her comment but moved back toward my vehicle.

"So… I promised you could see me on my birthday… see me?!? Now I gotta get to the store and head back home for the night."

They both said they loved me, and I just started up the 1997 Isuzu Rodeo I had bought for just such occasions. Then I gave them my standard response,

"You too."

There was a legion of kids that wandered our neighborhood. I found them crawling like fleas all over our ramp when I got home.

"Hey! No playing after dark tonight!" I barked.

Among the chorus of "awwwwws" and "Pleeeeeases" the sassy voice of the eldest girl in the group rang out,

"Are you boys gonna Paaaar-tay tonight?!", followed by a wave of snickering and giggling.

"No playing after dark! Or I will tell your parents every terrible thing we've ever caught y'all doin' over here!"

The kids ranged from five to fifteen. The high school aged ones seemed far more threatened and quickly wrangled their younger siblings back home.

I wasn't landed an hour before Mom called.

"I can't believe you didn't tell me you were getting a dog!"

"Um, Sorry…"

"Why don't you get one from Pete's rescue?"

"Because Pete works in a factory now, and I want a Pit-"

"Pit-bulls are so mean Mark! They're always on the news!

What if he eats one of those kids!? Most places won't even allow them; have you even asked your property owners?"

Mom had put herself through school with a scholarship and was a teacher. Dad had put himself through law school by auctioneering and was an attorney. When they got together and talked about kids, they chased each other down a bottomless rabbit hole of worst-case scenarios that had always led to lectures like this from one or the other.

"Gotta go Liz! Guests are arriving!"

I popped the tab on the evening's first drink and played video games until the guests started arriving. It had always been dream of mine to make a video game. After a few years working in corporate technology, I became very content to stick with playing them.

At the party, I told Tom I was taking a pup. His eyes got big as he told me about his first few months with his boy.

"Six feet of drywall bro, studs had to be replaced too. We left him alone to go see a movie and came back to six feet of drywall turned into powder and the studs turned into toothpicks!"

Jude and Mary were happy I was getting a pup but had their own motives for being that way.

"Our boys need someone to play with!! We'll help you train it!" Mary said.

Jude turned a sarcastic grin toward Mary's offer of training. "To do what, eat and sleep on the couch all day?!"

As the evening wound down, I cornered Peter. He rarely gave an opinion you didn't ask for and even at that there was usually a measured reluctance in the way he delivered his thoughts.

"Am I biting off more than I can chew with a Pit? Pun

intended."

"Pit-bulls are the most loyal breed I've come across; they will do anything for the people they love… literally anything. If an owner wants its Pit to be vicious, that dog's gonna be a killer, if an owner wants a couch-potato, that dog's gonna be a pillow."

"What about me, what kinda owner do you think I'll be?"

He measured his response.

"If it's like in our game group… When someone stands in fire, you get instantly irritated. I worry the pup won't have time to figure out what 'fire' is before you wanna ship it off to the shelter."

"That does annoy me when people just stand and burn!"

"Sometimes it may not be their fault, maybe they got lag or kids screaming in the back room. Everybody is playing their character the best they can. We're all tryin' to improve on our weaknesses and build on our strengths… I do think a dog could maybe help you improve at least one of your weak points."

"Which one?"

"Patience."

"Speaking of the games, how much longer before we get new raid content?! I feel like we've been fighting the same battles forever!"

The morning Ben called to say the litter was out, I thought I had everything ready for my new little boy. Bowls, food, a box of toys. I'd found a length of small-link chain in our junk pile that I thought would look tough as a first collar. For a bed, I had the weathered blanket I'd picked up at an Arizona truck stop on the bus ride back from California so many years before. Ben was uncharacteristically unsure of himself.

"It was a litter of six, Cuz. Can you and Pete swing by today? I just want him to make sure everything looks good. I don't know how this is all supposed to go…"

He had gotten his little girl right after coming home from his last trip over to Afghanistan. You could tell he had been worried about her the whole time she was carrying. He didn't worry much so, in a way, it was refreshing to see.

"I'll be sure and bring him man, we'll swing by right after work."

When Peter and I got there, Ben was outside watching over the litter. His girl just looked up at us with this overwhelmed face and went right back to figuring out how to be a mother to these six little fur-balls clawing and biting at her.

I looked over to Ben and asked which ones were boys. His prideful smile turned to a grin of amusement.

"Six girls Cuz, get Pete to check… but I'm seeing six girls down there."

I figured the odds on that were impossible. Peter made his way into the cage and negotiated with their mama for approval to check them out. Disappointment came rolling in as he looked up, bewildered and grinning. I didn't even let him speak,

"Ain't that a bitch!"

"A whole litter of 'em!! They all look healthy, even this little runt. It's a good litter to pick from." Each word worked into the rhythm of his chuckling.

"How's their mama doin' Pete?"

"She looks great man. Drained, of course, but she looks to be taking it like a champ."

"Word! When I saw it was only six and no boys, I got worried there might be one stuck or something."

"Nah man, first litters are usually smaller, she's all done."

I had been dead set on getting a boy. As they were talking about what Ben should expect in the coming weeks, I was thinking it must be a sign that I didn't need a dog.

"You know which one you want Cuz?"

"I really wanted a boy man, not sure what I wanna do now."

He pointed to a monster of a pup plowing through her littermates like a bulldozer.

"Right there's your meanest, biggest too."

And then, there was the runt. As they all wrestled for their spots at the dinner table, the little runt gave everything she had, but she just kept getting pushed off, stepped on, and outright disrespected by her sisters.

When they all finished eating, they gathered themselves into a mass of fur under their mama's belly. The runt crawled her way out of the heap and got right up next to her mother's face, where she curled up and let her mama rest on her like a pillow.

Peter could tell I was discouraged.

"Girls are easier to raise, it might be good for your first dog to be a girl."

"I'm gonna think on it man, I just know my luck with girls."

I made several trips to Ben's over the next six weeks. Tom rode with me a time or two, getting more tempted to keep one with each trip. He remembered how much his little boy had cost him and by week four, he was done visiting.

"We can't afford another one bro! I'm just teasing myself over here. Ben, I'll help you get rid of them when they're ready."

"Another two weeks and they should be good."

"Just let me know!"

I'd never been around puppies and had no immunity to

their cuteness. The big one got bigger, the four in the middle did well, and the runt did her best to keep up. We tried to spread our attention evenly between them, but I found myself feeling more and more sorry for that little runt every trip. She could never fight her way through her sisters to be the first one picked up. I started making it a point to pass them all over for her, and instead of the nips and scratches her sisters re-paid my attention with, she just licked my hands and face until her turn was over. When I sat her down, she took the opportunity to have her mama and the food pan to herself.

The weekend before he was planning to give the pups away in a parking lot, Ben hit me with news.

"I think I'm going back in the Service, Cuz. I'm gonna re-enlist."

"What made you change your mind? I thought you were done after that last tour."

"A lot of things… a lot of thinkin', maybe too much thinkin'."

When 9/11 happened, Ben enlisted. He had spent about 6 years of his life going back and forth to war, but after his last trip, something had changed.

"Seriously man, why go back now?"

"I just feel like I was born to fight, like it's what I was made for and where I belong. I'm wanna get into special ops. I'm 'bout to be too old to even apply… so, it's time… y'know?"

In all that talk, I was picturing Ben as a commando character from one of the many games I'd played. I could totally see him doing all that for real, being the hero that I could only ever pretend to be.

"Well man, I've always been proud of you for serving, but this is next level. Honestly, I'm stoked for ya."

He smiled like when we were kids, a smile I thought he'd lost in the sand.

"I appreciate that Cuz, you'll prob'ly be the only one. On that note, don't mention it to anyone. I don't know how or when I'm gonna break it to the family. Mama was getting used to not having to worry about me."

"What about the mama in there?" I pointed to the pen.

"Haven't figured that out yet. I might send her to my dad's, he's got land. We gotta get them pups gone first. Did you make up your mind if you want one yet? I see you favoring that runt."

"She is a sweetheart…"

"I'll call you before they go, even if you don't take her, you should at least say goodbye."

He called the day before they were going. I went out to the pen, and we went through our routine. The runt gave me licks and went back to her mom; the rest gave me their last loving wounds. Ben went back inside, and I went to my ride.

When I sat down to go, I looked back at the pen where all the pups were scavenging for spilled kibble. All except the little runt. She was yipping, howling, and jumping; trying to climb the fence, and staring straight at me with desperation in her eyes. Her howling bark sounded like a whistle screaming,

'Don't leave me! Dooooon't leeeeeave meeeee!'

I was out of the Rodeo and up to the kennel before I realized what I was doing. Ben was already walking from his patio toward the cage. He barely had it open and that little brat wiggled out and charged at me with her tail wagging in a blur and her tongue flapping in the wind. She made it to my feet and started clawing my pants and trying to climb me like a tree.

"Did you wanna say goodbye again sweetheart? I'll miss

you too, but you'll find a good home!"

I picked her up and she clamped onto my shirt with her teeth and locked her eyes onto mine; Ben looked over with a big grin.

"So… what's her name Cuz?"

"I think I'm gonna name her Karma."

"Karma?!"

"Yeah Karma… Cause Karma's a bitch."

I got in the Rodeo and sat her over in the passenger seat. She slid up against the back and found 'her' spot. I started up the engine and gave her another look. I had no idea how these few pounds in my passenger seat were about to change my life, but she had convinced me to find out. I put us in gear and gave her a pat on her head.

"Let's get you home Sweetheart."

Chapter Two

I was the only one surprised when I came home with a puppy. Those first three days were all carrying her around to meet her family and my friends. Nana was thrilled I'd gotten a pup; Grace didn't know what to think, but in her defense, Karma was trying to nurse off her.

One of the sweetest moments I had ever seen in my life up to that point was when my buddy's 6-year-old daughter curled up in the floor with Karma and laid a blanket over them both before falling asleep. There was something in that moment I hadn't felt before then, a new kind of warmth and pride.

Jude and Mary's pups were mostly jealous of all the attention their parents gave my runt. I felt like that was my vengeance on them for stealing my friends and ended my vendetta against dog-kind.

When it came time to meet Mom and Dad, Karma was a perfect angel. She was giving kisses and making cute puppy grunts. Mom started rubbing her ears and Karma fell right to sleep in her lap.

"She feels like velvet!" Mom whispered.

We talked about who we'd met, what shots she needed, and where she was going to stay, then Karma woke up and gave a few yips. I'd learned pretty quick that I could spend my time outside with my dog or I could spend that same time inside, cleaning up her mess. I took every sound she made under a roof to mean that she had to potty and went to collect her from Mom's lap.

"Can I take her out?" Mom asked.

"Sure, just stay close to her – she's faster than you'd think."

They made their way outside and Dad asked how I was doing.

"I'm hangin' in there; it's not been as tough as I thought."

"I recall saying something similar when we brought you home. Just you wait!"

"How's the breakfast club? Nana told me one of your charter members was sick?"

"We're all getting older, but we still convene every morning over coffee to solve the world's problems."

"You guys have been at it since I was a kid… You come up with any anything yet??"

Mom and Karma broke-up our father-son talk to report that Karma had pottied as she sat her down. Karma took to chasing her tail, slipping and falling every time she caught it, which got us all to laughing. It sounded foreign, the three of us laughing together, like it was coming from the TV or a neighbor's house.

After our good moment, I felt like it was time to move on, before some random argument broke out, as tended to happen on my visits.

In that first week, Karma balanced her time between the food bowl and sleeping under my chair while I played video games. When bedtime came, I would lay down on the futon mattress I had on the floor, she would curl up by my feet, and then she would snore until I got up. By the end of week two, it seemed like I had everything under control. All the worry and concern about getting a dog had been for nothing.

But no. The adorable cotton-ball of affection and love transformed into a spiteful row of teeth with legs and claws. She just wanted to whine and bark and chew. She chewed everything. Trash, clothes, furniture, the carpet; anything she saw, she wanted to chew. And if something scared her; she ran right toward it, mouth open, ready to chew.

The cat, Nubs as she'd come to be called, was the only thing that had any hope of surviving alone. In addition to having no tail for Karma to chase, Nubs had also come equipped with claws. Karma would plop down next to her and bare her mouthful of pearly needles. Then, without a sound, Nubs would throw three quick swats at Karma's nose, sending the mutt yelping through the house. Nubs was back to sleep before Karma finished her first stride.

Every third word out of my mouth was 'no'.

"No chewing shoes", "No chewing beds", "NO CHEWING ELECTRICAL CABLES!"

"No chewing doors", "No chewing chairs", "NO CHEWING PEOPLE!"

No. Nooooo. No! No… NO!!

She would look up at me and yowl in defiance, then chew at the air and growl.

Karma also loved to eat. She had this resolve melting magic trick of tilting her head back and making her eyes double in size if she found you eating something she wanted to try. It was irresistible if she caught you in her pitiful stare. She loved to play too, but preferred cardboard to any of the toys we had for her. Finally, we just decided to let her chew boxes. She would hold them down with her paws and growl and rip and tear until the whole thing was in shreds. I looked on, imagining how bad that would be if she were full grown and it was one of the neighborhood kids instead of a box. Right behind food and cardboard, Karma loved praise. Her eyes lit up and she smiled every time she heard 'Good Karma!', unfortunately she didn't earn a lot of praise in the beginning.

She started exploring more; dandelions were a particular fascination. When she sniffed at them, all the little seeds would blow away and she would chase after them trying to chomp them all. Everything was full of wonder for her. She jumped at every sound, marveled at every bug and blade of grass. The more she saw, the braver she got, and the harder it became to keep up with her energy. Then, she started getting the zoomies.

When she was asleep, she was still that innocent, adorable ball of fur that wouldn't let me leave her to be adopted by a stranger. That kept just enough patience in the tank to keep us together.

Peter got a crate from his old job, and we set it up in the laundry room. Karma had been roaming free in the house for about a month, so the first time we put her in there she was curious. We gave her a half-dozen toys and some cardboard, then we all left the house for a day trip. When we shut the door, it seemed like she was content.

When we came home that night, you could hear her shrieking from two houses away. We opened the door to find her curled up in the back of the cage, shaking like a leaf, making a mournful whistling sound. She saw us and her whine fell to a grunty whimper as she crawled toward us with her head low and tail tucked. We let her out and she slowly came and laid down at our feet, then put her chin on the toe of my shoe and turned her little brown eyes up at us. I swear, they were filled with tears. I felt like a terrible person and looked to Peter for reassurance that I wasn't.

"With all the traffic through this place, I bet she's never been alone before."

"Nubs was here!"

"… I bet Nubs spent every second laughing at her from outside the cage. Karma may have been better off alone."

She never really took to the cage. Anytime we put her in it, she would scream and wail until we let her out. As the extra links on her chain collar quickly went from three, to two, to one, she became even more of a handful with our frequent guests. She jumped on them, chased them, demanded their attention; she even went to the bathroom right in front of them. They were good sports and we rarely excluded Karma from the goings on in that house. One exception was when a band practiced. We always locked her up for that. All those instrument cables swinging around were just long tempting tails for her to chase. Luckily, the amplifiers were loud enough to drown out her protests.

My patience with everything was thin in month three. When Robert called to check in, I couldn't help but recall how much of an angel I remembered his dog had been when I met her. He and I worked together downtown and rented a house together for a while before I'd fled to California. It was like a big-city version of Peter's party house. Robert had moved out and got his pup when living with a constant flow of people and peril in and out of our place became too much. I'd circled the drain for a while after that before giving it all up.

"Whassup little bro, how do I sound?"

"Umm, same as you've always sounded…"

"Oh… well I'm calling you from a smartphone, I was

wondering if I sounded any smarter."

At the time, smartphones seemed like another tech fad to me.

"Um okay, that's cool… Hey, I got a dog!"

"Whaaaat?!?! What kind"

"She's a Pit"

"Are there any walls left in your house?!?!"

"So far… She's nothin' like I remember your angel being though, she's a monster!!"

"Ha! My girl was the Angel of Death! Every time I let her out, she came back with something dead, and if I didn't let her out, she would try to kill my stuff! It was at least a year before she got like she was when you met her. Give your girl time. So, you still living at that house with your brother?"

"Yeah man, same place."

"I'm gonna be up that way for a bit next week, tons of our servers are running systems from Y2K and support ends soon. Work is moving me up north for a couple of years to sort out compatibility issues. I'm wanting to catch up with all my friends around here while they're still less than a day away. Would it be cool if I drop in and check on ya?"

"I can't believe anything from Y2K is still a thing… For sure man, all are welcome here."

"Awesome! I'll give you a shout when I get to town, then we'll pin it all down. And say, you let me know if you wanna come back to tech work. We're hiring!"

"No thank you, had all I could stand of being a cog in that machine."

"Well, standing offer, if you should change your mind. You're missing out, I'm making money hand over fist with this gig!"

Robert walked in with his smartphone held high. He passed it around for everyone to see and we all admired this thing that looked like it had come off an intergalactic starship. The moment I understood what it meant to be a dog owner was later, when Peter found Robert's new toy looking more like something that fell off a UFO after it crashed into Earth at 17,000 miles per hour.

Peter had arrested the culprit and chained her to the ramp as soon as he discovered the crime. Her howling echoed in the bell-shape of the half-pipe, and was almost as loud as her victim, who was engaged in pounding out a classic rock cover on the drums with our regulars in the jam room.

When Peter handed it to me, I wasn't even sure what I was looking at, then I realized. I saw the signature ice pick wounds, the drying residue of the vandal's slimy drool. I saw the whole crime play out in my mind and knew. It was Karma. Peter looked baffled as he surveyed the wreckage.

"I don't know how she got it or, honestly, how she did THIS much damage. She's still so little…"

My replies were mostly dirty words.

That little monster had destroyed tons of things since I brought her home, but nothing like this.

"I'll deal with it when the band takes a break. In the meantime-"

I tried my best to sound like the responsible father of a problem child,

"I'm going to have a talk with Karma."

As I made my way to the door, evidence in hand, I started deciding what I meant by 'talk'. Nubs was sleeping on top of the laundry we'd piled on Karma's cage. She woke up long enough to cut me a glare of cruel amusement and turned her attention back to sleep.

I was so mad. I was thinking 'I am gonna hold this thing right in her face and shout 'BAD KARMA!', and I'm gonna whip her with this belt I'm wearing!' I'm not sure I knew that anger was a secondary emotion back then, but I knew it was primarily what I was feeling it.

I started fiddling with my belt buckle just outside the door.

'And she's sleeping outside from now on! Liz and Dan are right; dogs shouldn't be in the house!' I thought.

I got to the tethered defenseless vandal, and I threw that scrap of a phone down at her and shouted:

"NO!! BAD KARMA!"

The snap of the belt to her backside cracked into the night, and to my complete surprise, it hurt… me.

My arms sank as she turned her brown eyes up. I couldn't believe how confused they looked, how sorry she looked, how much apology I heard in her whine. It was like, she didn't know what she had done, but she knew it had really hurt me and she was deeply sorry. I felt awful about the phone, awful about what I had just done to her, awful about where I was in life, just awful about everything. I saw this frustrated, angry person reflecting back at me in her pitiful pit-bull eyes and wondered how I'd become that guy. I wondered if she would have been better off with one of those strangers, away from all this chaos and confusion. Away from me. Then:

"WHERE is my PHONE!"

Lost in my reflections on why I had brought this fuzzy destruction into my life, I hadn't heard the band stop playing or noticed Karma chewing on the world's new favorite toy again. She looked up at me and I snatched the phone out from under her paw.

"No chewing expensive electronic things that I can't afford

to replace. Bad Karma."

She sat up to attention and gave me a clear-eyed look that said, 'Got it!'

As I walked toward my fate, I yelled back to remind her of her own.

"YOU'RE STILL MOVING OUTSIDE!"

It wasn't pretty. I explained what happened, we shouted for a bit, he said my dog needed a beating and started stamping toward the door. I grabbed his shoulder while shouting that he was the one about to get a beating, and he whirled around with fire in his eyes and his fists in the air. We took it outside. Very quickly, we were back inside, Robert with a cotton ball jammed into his busted nose and me with my busted lip making it hard to talk. We called it a draw. We were both smiling, laughing, and slapping each other on the back - both pretending our eyes were watering from taking punches and not from how ashamed we felt for throwing them.

Karma stayed outside and let no one forget she was out there. For miles around, everyone knew Karma was out there.

Her pleas became more desperate as the night wore on and we reduced her sentence from 'moving' outside to 'staying one night' outside. Everyone agreed not to let her in, no matter how annoying it got. And yet, somehow, I woke up with that filthy mutt beside me.

I reached over to pet her and saw the dirt on her fur move to my arm like I was a magnet. It was fleas. She was covered. It looked like millions of them crawling through her white fur. We had noticed the neighborhood strays camping under our ramp and, apparently, that made it a hotbed of flea activity in the area.

I ran her to the tub and started washing her down. She was

flailing around on the fiberglass, trying to stand up and play, thrilled to be in the house, and even more thrilled by the discovery of hot water. She had drenched my clothes, so I just jumped in the tub with her, and we ran armies of fleas down the drain.

When we got back to bed, she was shivering from being wet, or possibly from blood loss, I don't know – but she abandoned her usual spot by my feet and worked her way under the covers to curl up by my chest. I could feel her heart beating. I told her she was a good girl and just had a bad day, that we would try again tomorrow. I put my arm around her and she let out a gentle, easy sigh. Then, she started snoring. Loudly.

Slowly, she was learning to resist the urge to chew. She would approach your hand with her mouth wide open, ready to chomp, but more and more, instead of trying to chew your hand, she would just give you a lick or two. You could clearly see the struggle in her eyes.

The video store cut my hours and I had more time to work with her. She'd picked up the nickname 'cardboard' for learning to sit, lay down, play dead, and roll-over in exchange for scraps of cardboard. And then came her finale, Twirl.

She would jump up in the air and try her best to spin all the way around, then land facing you again. Most often, she landed on her own face. Still, her commitment to that trick was complete, no fear of failure or pain. No matter how often she failed, she gave 'twirl' 100%, every time. She was thrilled when she landed it, and she was just as thrilled when she fell and made us laugh. It led me to teasing Jude about how boring his dogs were. He dismissed it.

"You can't teach an old dog new tricks, dude."

"I hope that's not true, man, you and I are fast becomin' old dogs."

He and Mary were about to move to Colorado to level up her Nursing career. They asked if we could keep their dogs while they went out to scout around. I agreed and they dropped their boys off later that week. We had couches everywhere. There were couches in the living room, couches in the kitchen, couches outside. It took them a while to find their favorite. Karma, although she was trying to be helpful, made it worse. Everywhere they went, she was right there.

'Do you need anything?'

'Do you wanna play?'

'Do you need company?'

'I can do tricks!'

The boys got a bit grumpy with her so I pulled her attention away for the afternoon. Aside from trips outside, everyone did their own thing that night. The next morning, the pack and I got up for our morning routine of making coffee, practicing Karma's tricks, and then having breakfast.

Jude had left jerky treats for the boys. I pulled a piece for Karma and asked her to sit. Her tail thundered to the ground for the jerky.

"Lay down"

She shook the house dropping into position. All we ever gave her was cardboard and a 'Good Karma!' for rewards. She could have felt cheated by discovering that there were things called 'dog treats' and usually, doing tricks got you one, but it just inspired her to do better.

The boys stepped forward and looked at me with interest. I held out another treat and said 'sit'. Karma illustrated the move for them. In much less dramatic fashion, the younger pup cautiously sat and I gave him a treat. The older followed his lead and flopped his tail to the ground. I gave Karma an extra treat for being teacher's assistant.

"He may not be able to teach an old dog new trick, but Karma can! Good Karma!"

Jude and Mary got back on schedule; I hadn't said anything about the tricks. They had left us a couple of couch-potato pups and as the boys ran through our routine, the pride on Mary's face was radiant. Jude just looked confused, as if what he saw challenged a basic assumption he held about the universe. After the show, they were both excited to get back home with their fur-babies. Karma said farewell, with customary tail sniffs for dogs and face licks for people, showing no real concern for what order that happened in.

When I was growing up, Thanksgiving was the big family event. Attendance had been spotty in the years since my grandfather passed, but with Ben's news having reached all our kin, it was looking like that year would be a full house.

I carpooled with Peter to Nana's for the feast. We opened her door and stepped into the past. The chill in the air was blown back by the warmth of her house. Hints of sage, rosemary, and thyme lingered on the fading aroma of onions, garlic, and roasting turkey. Behind that was the growing buttery scent of apples and cinnamon with sugary wisps of peanut brittle coming to a boil. We all told Ben how proud we were. More quietly, we told each other how much we worried. I caught him alone out in the backyard, where we had made most of the memories we shared.

"I'm headed back to your old stompin' ground Cuz, you need to come hang out."

"San Diego? Good luck with those waves man, I went out there thinkin' I was gonna surf my days away in a California dream. Yeah, no. The first time I got in the water with a board, this huge wall of ice-water rolled me a mile across the rocks and sand. I came up for a gasp of air, and it hit me with another one that rolled me to shore and I took the hint."

"I heard it's rough!"

"Freezing! Nothin' like the Gulf."

Nana interrupted our conversation with a call for dessert, and the family broke off into its factions to enjoy sweets and gossip. Then, car by car, everyone made their way back to the lives they had built since moving out from under Nana's roof. Ben helped me carry the trash to the can.

"Man, what was it they used to yell at you about havin' a goal?" I asked.

"They'd say, 'If you don't have a goal, you don't have a soul'."

"That was it!"

"Everything is harder without a goal Cuz, even just making your bed. You should make a goal to come hang out when I get settled. Karma is welcome too!"

"I've spent a lot of time thinkin' about life lately, but I don't feel like I've spent much time living it… I guess I've just got some unresolved feelings about my past that I can't… well… get past."

"Unresolved feelings are like unexploded ordinance; they tend to blow up on innocent people."

"Ugh, maybe I need therapy or something."

"Grandpap said never trust your heart to someone you gotta pay… That's what I thought when I went but after a few sessions, it helped. One thing for sure, if you're gonna change, you're gonna have to give something up, it's just a law of nature."

"Maybe one day I'll get into that. In the meantime, an

adventure sounds like exactly what I need. Let me know when you get set up and I'll try to come visit."

"Word!"

I shared my thoughts with Peter on the way home, especially my concerns about not wanting to travel with Karma. He said he'd be more than happy to babysit. By the time we got home, the dream had started to grow, my first in a long while. A drive across the country, coast-to-coast. Something to save for and look forward to, just a reason to make my bed in the morning.

Chapter Three

Ever since Peter got his first job, Christmas had become a dull affair. We both bought everything we wanted throughout the year and our wish list was only ever one thing. Money. We used it to pay off all the stuff we'd put on our credit cards the year before. That first Christmas with Karma was different.

Nubs was expecting kittens and looked like a furry balloon on Christmas eve. Karma knew something was going on and hovered over her like a mother hen, despite Nubs' constant swatting and hissing. When Mom invited Karma to Christmas, it seemed like a good opportunity to get her out of the house and let Nubs have an evening's peace for the holiday. I agreed, despite my concerns about what hundred-year-old piece of furniture might finally end its long run on earth.

We arrived at sunset on Christmas eve. Karma was ecstatic to see Mom and Dad, who had been slowly warming up to the idea that, maybe, Pit-bulls weren't so bad. As Karma charged in the house, my memories of Peter and I damaging a choice antique when we were young sent chills down my spine.

We all gathered around the table to eat, the folks asked about Nubs, our friends, and what we had planned for the new year. We heard the jingle of a little bell on the Christmas tree, and I noticed Karma was missing. Before I could get to the living room, it was already far too late.

The most excited child that ever lived could not have torn open presents any faster or with more conviction, passion, and enthusiasm than Karma did when she got a hold of everyone's gifts that night. I shouted out,

"Bad Karma!" But Mom put her hand on my shoulder.

"Don't. Just let her open them."

Present by present she went, holding each one between her paws and tearing the brightly colored paper away, then ripping open the cardboard and laying its contents aside. We were in tears at the look of achievement on her face. After each present, she looked at us like it was the best gift ever given. I remembered home movies of being a kid and feeling excited to open gifts. I could tell, Karma felt like that or better, and my folks felt like parents again. It was the best Christmas we'd had since Grandpap died.

Karma got anxious on the way back home. When we opened the door, she started whining and charged to the kitchen couch. Nubs had crawled back behind it and was in the early stages of litter-labor. I got Karma settled and our things put away while Peter refined Nubs' nursery. We got the cleanup supplies ready, queued up some records, and delivered some kittens for Christmas.

We woke up with a litter of three kittens, a worn-out mommy, and an overstuffed puppy. Karma looked like roadkill beside the bed. I left her to sleep it off and went to check the litter. Peter was inspecting the kittens, two calicos with no tails and one tabby with a long tail. We wished each other a Merry Christmas and called our friends to do the same, casually offering them a kitten for the occasion.

Eventually we heard the slow clacking of Karma staggering down the hall. She was the picture of holiday excess; bloated and bleary-eyed, stumbling and utterly spent. Still, she made her way over to Nubs and gave each kitten a sniff and a lick before finding a spot to lay down and keep watch.

We spent that day on the couches in our kitchen. Nubs sorted out motherhood and Karma did her best to keep an eye on her new brother and sisters.

After one day of motherhood, Nubs' patience with Karma wore out and we decided to start putting her outside with the neighborhood kids all day. They were more interested in their new toys than her, so she dug a nest under the ramp and laid there until I came to get her. On her way back in, she gave the new litter a quick check and made her way to bed for the night.

We were all looking forward to New Year's Eve, but as the night approached, Karma seemed like she didn't feel that well. At first, we thought it was dejection over Nub's not letting her near the kittens, then she started throwing up and we thought it was all the leftovers she'd been eating. The night of the party, she was a no-show, choosing to spend the whole night curled up on the pile of laundry in the bottom of my closet.

I woke up feeling awful. There was a putrid smell in the room and the visuals on what Karma had left in my floor are unrepeatable. Within minutes, Peter had caught wind of it and professed with all authority.

"That's wrong!"

I paid more attention to my headache and churning stomach than to his comment. He was right though, it was wrong. And it was everywhere. Peter stood there watching Karma play dead on the floor. She was following us with her eyes but never moved a muscle.

"That's wrong brother, something's wrong."

"Her stomach hasn't been right since Christmas, it's prob'ly just that mess clearing out."

"Man, I'm tellin' you, that is not a smell you want coming from your dog, back at the shelter that was the smell of a lot of spots about to open up."

I looked at Karma and called her name. I snapped my fingers and told her to sit up. Her eyes said she wanted to do as I'd asked but her body wouldn't let her. My heart sank.

"What should I do?"

"I think it's Parvo, if we can't get her to a vet today then-"

His eyes finished the sentence as they sank.

We found an emergency vet over an hour away; they were charging two months' rent just to look at her and basically told me that if it was Parvo, they'd end her suffering. When I came back inside, I found a fresh, more horrifying, mess from Karma and she was missing from her spot on my floor. I searched around and found she had crawled behind the same couch where Nubs had the kittens and was softly whimpering with each breath, like she didn't want to be heard or worry anyone. I had never seen a thing suffer like that or felt so completely helpless. I decided the only thing I could do was end her suffering. I found Peter outside.

"Will your pistol do it clean?"

He was searching through his phone and stopped in his tracks.

"Yes… But you should let the folks say goodbye first and you should give me at least another hour to try and get Doc on the phone, he owes me one."

I somberly consented and went back to Karma. I sat apologizing for thinking about travelling without her, and for that time I let fleas try to eat her alive. I told her it was alright that she'd eaten Robert's smartphone, that those things seemed like trouble anyway, and she was probably right to break it. I told her I loved her, and that I was so glad she had picked me.

In the middle of this moment we were having, my folks walked in. Dad took one look and turned away to head back outside, Mom reached back to pet her, and Karma let out a long whistling whine at the touch. That broke me. I went outside to request the gun again and found Peter on the phone. Dad was by the car with a ponderous look on his face as he eavesdropped on Peter's conversation.

"Sick puppy in there." He said as he shook his head.

I just nodded.

Peter hung up and reported that Doc agreed, it sounded like Parvo.

"He thinks it's day two or three and gave her 1 in 10 odds of making it without treatment. With an extended vet stay and a month of after care, maybe fifty-fifty based on where she at now. He said if we want, he'll meet us there and start treating her at once."

I had made up my mind before I'd come outside. Thinking about keeping Karma in that condition for a coin toss didn't sway it much.

"How much to put her down?" I asked.

"No! We are TAKING her!"

All eyes turned toward the door and found Mom holding a near lifeless Karma, in her arms, wrapped in a blanket. With absolute resolution, she demanded.

"We're taking her! We're not debating it, we're not discussing it, we are taking this sick baby to the doctor, and he is going to help her get better!"

"Liz..." I started; in the condescending tone I took with her back then.

"NO!" The word forced a river of tears from her eyes. "Get in a car or get out of my way, this poor baby is going to the doctor."

Mom hadn't moved, the tears streaming out of her eyes had run makeup down her cheeks and onto her collar, her voice trembled in time with Karma's failing breath. Karma peeked out of the blanket Mom had wrapped her in; her eyes found mine and I felt it, I knew I had to do everything I could to give her a chance, no matter how hard it was or how bad the odds were.

Mom got in the back of the Rodeo with Karma. Peter and Dad went in the folks' car.

When we got to the vet, Mom handed Karma to me and walked toward the clinic. Peter met her halfway and she almost collapsed on him. I looked down at Karma, her every breath a struggle and leaving her with a soft plea for help. Dad came to the window and said they were getting a quarantine ready still; they'd let us know when to bring her in, then he went back inside.

I talked to Karma. I told her that if she could find a way through this for me, I would take her on a road trip and we would go coast-to-coast, maybe even try to see all the states, if she just stayed in this world with me. I told her about people I'd left behind or lost and how glad I was she was with me. I told her I didn't want to lose her, and promised I'd never, never leave her. I apologized for thinking about not adopting her and for wishing she'd been a boy.

As best I could, without moving her too much, I held her face up and touched her nose to mine. Almost in slow motion, she gave me the lightest lick and let out a long sigh. Her eyes closed and her breath seemed to slow. I didn't know whether she was dying or resting but she seemed to be in less pain, and we sat there waiting.

Peter came back to say they were ready. As soon as I found the door handle, I lost the strength to pull it. Peter reached in through the window to my shoulder.

"I got her, brother."

I held Karma up and told her I was sorry, but if she ever wanted to see me again, she was going to have to make it through this.

I was ashamed of not being able to walk her in and get her set up. When Peter came back to the Rodeo, he came back to the driver's side.

"Let me drive."

"What'd he say?"

"Fifty-fifty brother, he is sure it is Parvo. He said he'd let us know as soon as he feels like it's moving one way or the other."

"Her pain?"

"There's not a lot they can do for that, but he said she's taking it well and thinks she's got a strong will to live."

By the time we got home, I wondered if Karma was even still alive, I worried she may have given up when we all abandoned her. For all I knew that little lick she'd given me was the last bit of energy she had, and she had used it for a kiss.

The emptiness of the house the next morning was stunning. Three kittens mewing, two roommates shuffling, and somehow Karma's absence still made the place feel desolate. Doc said she was responding better than expected and he would go ahead and give her 6 in 10 odds. I asked about her pain. He said she was hurting, but she'd won over the whole staff and the extra attention seemed to be helping.

On the wall above my bed was a map of the country with a

pin for every place I had already been. I spent the day adding places me and Karma were going to see. Every day after, I worked on that map and called the vet for updates. The second day he gave her 7 in 10, the third it was 9 in 10. On day four, he finally said it,

"You can come pick her up."

I went to get her alone. They had me come into the side entrance and stand in an area marked off with yellow tape. I heard the hard pounding of a tail against a metal crate and, by the rhythm, knew it was Karma. Three girls came around the corner, the one tech that had let me in was holding a fidgety, squirming Karma. She started to whine and struggle to get down when she caught sight of me. She had these huge sagging bulbous things all over her, the tech saw my concern and told me they were from saline bags they used to keep her hydrated during the treatment and that they'd go away.

They handed Karma over. She flopped into my arms, dug her claws into my shoulders, and pressed her head right up under my chin. I felt a warm sensation grow in my chest, and I couldn't remember feeling more relieved in all my life.

Looking up, I noticed all the techs were blushing and smiling, one girl had her mouth covered while she giggled. I thanked them all for taking care of my baby and after hearing their compliments for Karma, we were out the door.

Karma had woven herself into my shirt, every part of her clinging, pressing, or hanging on to me for dear life. We got to the Rodeo, and I lost it, I was so happy. I just kept telling her over and over how good she was, how she was the best girl.

I sat her in her spot and felt an icy chill in my chest. Then, I realized why the girls were blushing and why I had felt a warm sensation when they handed Karma over. She had thoroughly relieved herself all over me. I could not have cared less about my yellow stained t-shirt and I gave her another barrage of kisses and praise before we fired up the Rodeo.

I had to get Karma away from Peter's house until she fully recovered. The folks volunteered to set up an infirmary in their kitchen. It was a long run of teaspoons of water and kibble counted out like pills for Karma. We set up a crate and a table with all her meds on it and day after day, we all four took our turn doling out her spoons of water, bits of kibble, and pills. Karma would inhale the tiny bites of food, spit out the pills, and lap up water from a syringe with her eyes nearly popping out of her head, focused on not letting a single drop fall to waste, then she would look back at us confused, clearly wondering if she had survived Parvo for 'THIS?!'

When I finally went to bring her back home, Mom told me she'd promised Karma a birthday party during her recovery. I agreed a celebration was in order, and we set the date.

Karma came home to Nubs' kittens being into everything, as Karma had been when she was their age. The two calicos didn't want much to do with her, but the long-tailed tabby was curious when this big white beast came trotting into 'his' house and sniffed him over. Immediately, they were best friends. He was growing at a rate of about two-to-one over his siblings and had earned the name Big Bill.

Karma and Big Bill spent their days playing and cuddling, I spent mine working out our road trip plans. All the comings and goings in the house seemed to settle from an unpredictable ruckus into an orderly fun time. The neighborhood kids all clamored over Karma when we finally let her back out to play with them; all saying how excited they were to spend their summer break with her.

When her 1st birthday came, we just pretended she was a toddler. She was in an awkward lanky phase, where her legs looked longer than her body, but her height let her climb up onto seats somewhat gracefully. She climbed into a chair at the kitchen table while we all pretended not to watch. Too amused to pull her down, we sat around the table with Karma, in a chair, wearing a shiny party tiara that said 'Happy Birthday' on her head and a lei of purple, pink, and white fabric flower petals around her neck. When Mom pulled a little dog shaped cake from the fridge, I couldn't bring myself to stop her from giving Karma a piece.

It had been a long time since the four of us sat down for a meal together and didn't rattle on about life, our problems, the family, or our disagreements. Almost as if by magic, Karma took our minds off all that and we were just happy to be together.

Mom wrapped up gifts for 'Grammie's girl', as she called Karma now. After Karma was sure she'd destroyed all the paper and boxes, and that she hadn't missed anything edible, she showered her Grammie with kisses. Then, Mom pulled out two more packages. One, she gave to Karma, who opened it and found a bright red harness with a retractable leash to match. The harness had a bone shaped tag attached; engraved 'Karma', with my name and phone number below. In the smaller matching box, I found a pocket road atlas, inscribed: 'all roads lead home', and a keychain to match Karma's dog tag. Mine had my name and Mom's number. I got up and gave Mom a big hug with a long overdue "I love you", Karma joined in.

Chapter Four

Karma was getting bigger. She loved to play tug and it was amusing to see this little fur-beast snarling and pulling in vain at a length of rope we'd knotted up for her. After she pulled one of the kids off their feet, we had to teach Karma when to hold on, and when to let go.

It was a struggle at first, Karma had shown she was big into holding on – to me, to life, and to any toy she thought was hers. It was a summer-long battle of teaching her to 'let go!'. By the time the kids went back to school, she had a good sense of how hard she was supposed to pull, and when to turn loose.

Karma had to learn another lesson about letting go that fall. Dad had been right about his house, a lot of complicated things happened in the world and a lot of people lost a lot of money; most of them didn't really have it to lose. Every TV show on every channel was talking about it, and so were we. Through the raised voices and ill-informed opinions, Peter came solemnly in the door. Tom was the first to ask for his opinion on it all,

"Can you believe this mess, Bro?!"

Peter didn't even register Tom's question, he just looked at me.

"Big Bill got ran over… I just passed him on the highway."

The room went silent. For the brief time he'd been with us, Big Bill had proven himself a loveable oddity and source of constant entertainment. When Karma came trotting in, to welcome Peter home, he knelt to her level and said exactly what I was thinking,

"Karma, sweetheart, I'm sorry… Your best friend is dead."

Karma and Big Bill were nearly inseparable. He always kept an eye on her and was the first to welcome her home. If he wasn't with Karma, you were sure to find him with Peter.

Our Big Bill came home in a bag of thick black plastic. We dug him a hole and laid him down in it. Out of habit, or need, we said a few words. I said goodbye for Karma and thanked the plastic bag for being her friend. We each grabbed our shovels and filled in the hole. It seemed like Karma looked for her friend after that. She was restless for a couple of nights; she whined here and there. But life went on for her, and for all of us.

The first bomb we felt from the world's money problems landed on Tom. He made his living building houses and there were no houses being built. When he told the bank that he couldn't pay, they took his house. He had lived there with his girlfriend for years; that relationship was also lost in that blast.

We set him up on our finest couch and I assigned Nurse Karma to tend his wounds. He brought Karma's dad to the house with him, but his boy was an outdoor dog, so we gave him shelter in our garage with an old bench seat from a pickup truck to sleep on. He seemed happy with that, and with all the extra attention he got from having so many people come and go. I was happy Karma got to know her father, but sad about the events that led to the opportunity.

Tom mostly sat in front of our community computer and explored the world through a screen. Social media was still pretty new back then and he'd never had access to the internet, or even seen the need. But, in those days after his losses, he found it a welcomed distraction to bridge the gaps between his ever-scarcer repair and remodel jobs. He fixed up our place, did the same for other friends, but there wasn't much work or money so more than anything, he scrolled the web. Peter had gotten me a job at his factory once it was clear the video rental was a thing of the past and the video store was no longer reliable income. We tried to get Tom to join us, but he just scrolled the web.

Right before the holidays, Tom's brother called him up from Texas. He said he was opening a martial arts gym and needed help building out the place. There was a bed, family, and work to be done. Tom loaded up his things the day after the call.

"I hate to see ya go man, but I'm glad you got this opportunity."

"I appreciate y'all taking me in, bro. I'll be glad to return the favor if you and Karma wanna come hang out with us down there."

"For sure, I'm dead set on making that road trip happen next year, I promised Karma if she pulled through that Parvo thing we'd go."

"Just let me know!"

After a hug, we loaded his hundred-pound pup in his truck, and they were gone. Karma looked up at me with pitiful eyes wondering if everyone was always going to leave. Reaching down to rub her head I assured her,

"Don't' worry, we'll see them again."

Thanksgiving came and me and Peter made our way to our door, Karma routinely trotted toward her cage.

"We're gonna be brave this year Karma, we're gonna leave

you out while we're gone, and you're gonna be a good Karma… right?"

She sat down and smiled with her tongue hanging out. We both rubbed her ears and locked her in the house with Nubs, now free of her motherly duties and most often found at her favorite pastime: sleep.

There were several empty chairs around the table that year at Nana's, but everyone was talking about the mess of the world. It reminded me of being younger and everyone talking trash over a football game. This year was different, but very much the same…

"It's the red team!"

"It's the blue team!"

"It's dumb coaches!"

"It's lazy players!"

After dinner, the warring factions parted ways. It was the shortest gathering I could remember, but everyone thanked Nana, and she was grateful they had come. Peter and I stuck around to help clean up and I couldn't help but ask Nana how she felt and what she thought.

"All that matters is who ya love and who loves you in this world…"

She about got mad, but let it go with a sigh and digressed.

"I just wish people could get along and love each other…"

"We all love you, Nana!"

She gave me a big hug and gave Peter the same.

"And I love you boys! Will you be at the table next Thanksgiving, Sweetpea, or are you thinkin' you'll be out ramblin' with Karma?"

"I'm planning on being home for the holidays, but we'll see how it goes."

"Well, we'll save ya a plate, and you should bring Karma

with ya, her and Gracie can play in the garage."

"That sounds good Nana, we'll try to be here for that."

She gave us both another hug and buried us under tubs of leftovers. As we backed out her driveway she hollered

"I love you boys" and waved until we were out of sight.

Peter was frustrated about the whole night.

"I can't believe they couldn't just shut up and chew, it's Thanksgiving man, did you see Nana's face in all that?"

"Honestly, I was just tryin' to tune it out and pray that we still have a house when we get home."

"Karma? I bet she's fine, she really learned her boundaries this past year."

"If only people were so easy to teach, right?"

"Exactly!"

We came home to exactly the house we had left, with Karma and Nubs cuddled up on the couch.

"I'll miss you guys while you're gone." Peter confessed.

"I won't lie, it's hard to think about leaving in moments like this, but I feel that pull every day."

"I get it. I'm glad to see you moving in a direction that pulls you."

"Now seems like as good a time as any to bring it up; I'm thinkin' about moving to the folks' place after the first of the year."

"God help you."

"Do you think they'll let Karma live inside with me?"

"Not in a million years!"

"I was thinkin' the same. I'm thinkin' about setting up camp in their garage. I figure I could pull the Rodeo in to get it tuned up, and practice sleeping in a car and living on my portable stove and what-not. Assuming you don't mind me having to carpool to work with you."

"That sounds cool. You're welcome to stay here too. If you're just tryin' to cut expenses before you go, I'll cover your rent.'

"I think you've done enough of that brother, and I appreciate it. Truth is, it's been almost a year since I committed myself to this, and I've been moving in the right direction, but day-to-day, my life hasn't changed. I'm afraid I'm gonna put it off and I know if I move home, that'll light a fire under me."

"Any idea when you're planning on leaving?"

"Not yet. I was gonna bring it up to the folks at Christmas and work the plan out from there."

"Keep me posted brother, anything I can do to help, I'm here."

"I appreciate ya."

Karma woke from her slumber and gave us both a sniff for any table scraps we had brought her. There were none we were going to let her have. She hung her head in disappointment before moving to my bed.

"I think she's got the right idea. I'm gonna call it a night."

"Yeah, same here, I'll see you tomorrow man. Hey, the new expansion drops in a few weeks and Mom is asking what we want for Christmas – should I tell her to get that?"

"Yeah… I'm eager to play but I suppose waiting a month won't hurt."

"Sweet, I'll let her know."

In addition to the treat of watching Karma open her own presents for Christmas, the folks got to see me and Peter excited to open a present. Unfortunately for them, we were quick to get home and start playing our new game.

From Christmas to Valentine's Day, it was sleep, work, and games. Occasionally we ate. Poor Karma spent that whole winter under my chair, faithfully waiting for me to take a break from hunting down a young prince who had become a monster while trying to save his people. I just kept promising her,

"We'll get all our time together on the road, it'll just be me, and you, and the Rodeo. We can go wherever you want!"

She looked at me with believing eyes while I spent hour after hour in a virtual world. Then, one day, I looked at my bank account and it was full. I had saved up the money we needed. It was time.

In my excitement to get home to play my present, I hadn't brought up moving home to the folks at Christmas. I stopped by with Karma on one of the first warm days of that year and just asked.

"Can we move in for a while, to get ready for our trip?"

"Of course!"

"Can Karma stay inside with me?"

There was a silence as they passed glances back and forth to each other and Karma. Before they could form a response, I just shifted my request.

"Or would it be okay if we just stayed in the garage maybe? We can practice living out of a car."

Even at that, they seemed unsure how to respond, but Dad took the lead.

"That will be fine, if that's what you want to do."

I took the news back home and told Peter I would be moving out, planning to hit the road the day after my birthday. That left about two months to sort out all the details.

I started making calls. Robert was in Georgia, Tom was in Texas, Jude and Mary were settled in Colorado, and Ben felt like he would be ready for company in California by the end of the summer. Having those safehouses, we started working out the path we would take between them. We were going east to the Atlantic, then zigzagging across the lower half of the country to end up on the Pacific Coast in early fall. From there, we would head back home for the holidays and figure out what came next.

The roommates planned a big party for our last night in the house. With Jude, Mary, Ben, and Tom all gone, it felt like none of my close friends were there, but everyone was Karma's best friend and that made it special. We all swapped stories about things Karma had done or destroyed. We remembered Big Bill, and talked about how the neighborhood kids were growing up. Everyone looked at my map and asked questions about our trip. They all demanded I start a website or social media profile and post pictures of our travels.

I felt obligated to stay up until the last guest had left or found a place to pass out. When I was content to crash, I found Karma sprawled out and drooling all over my pillow. I pushed her over to make room for myself and we spent our last night in that room where our story began. I didn't sleep a wink.

It was two weeks until departure day. Peter wanted to take me to our favorite Chinese restaurant partly for my birthday and partly for a bon voyage.

We had frequented that restaurant for years. In all that time, I think the only thing we ever ordered was General Tso's chicken. That day was no different. We went back over my plans, remembered good times from the party house, our favorite server, a Chinese grandmother who said we were "just like her boys", brought our plate of ginger-laced spicy goodness to the table and we ate. After we'd finished devouring the velvety crimson chicken, she brought our check and fortune cookies. She asked if she could open them for us, which made us feel even more special. When she opened mine, she looked confused.

"ohhh nooo, It says 'Pain and Torture are in your future'."

My heart froze at the ill omen. When she handed the little slip of paper to me, I almost choked. It said, 'Fame and Fortune'. Peter and I waited until we got outside to break into side-splitting laughter. No sooner than we recovered ourselves, he broke into,

"I forgot to mention, Nubs has buns in the oven again."

'Good lord! Are you ever gonna get her fixed man?!"

"Yeah. Doc said to lock her up with this litter, and as soon as they're weaned, to bring her in and he'd take care of her. "

"Poor thing."

"I guess. So, what's left on your agenda before you go, brother?"

"I'm gonna swing by and see Nana tomorrow or the next day, then Mom wants to grill out on my birthday, and I'm planning on leaving out early that next morning. Aside from that, just sleep."

"I'll be at the cookout, but prob'ly just call to wish you godspeed the morning of though."

When we got back home, the folks and Karma were, shockingly, all curled up on the couch watching a movie.

"I know you're wanting to leave on your birthday, but Karma wants to wait until her birthday.'

"She doesn't know when her birthday is Mom, we can just double up for mine.'

"She might not know, but I do, and I want to have my little girl a 2nd birthday party."

The closer I had gotten to leaving, the more intimidating the road trip had become. I agreed, with one condition:

"No birthday cake this year for her, let's do birthday steak instead."

"Deal!" Mom cheered.

The next morning, I called to update people on the change of plans and went to see Nana. She was excited for me to take the trip, but nervous. She was glad I was going to see Ben.

"He's a long way from anyone who loves him, and in a dangerous line of work, I worry about him."

"I'll make sure he's doin' alright Nana; we'll even get some pictures of your grandsons on the beach."

"Don't forget my great granddog!"

"I won't Nana!"

"I worry about all you young'uns tryin' to find your way in this mean ol' world. I hope you can all remember nuthin' out there matters as much as what's in here."

She placed her hand over her heart.

"It is a great big world Nana, I guess part of the reason I wanna go on this trip is to find a home for my heart, it's restless here… But! You can bet I'll be back to my place at your table every chance I get."

"Reverend says gamblin' is a sin, but I'll bet your Grandpap's silver ring that your heart finds its home is right back here, 'round this table."

I told her we were waiting until Karma's birthday to leave and promised to stop by one more time before I left. I came back on my birthday, and she had a present for me. It was wrapped in plain brown paper. No bows or ribbons, no card.

"Happy birthday! I want you to take this with you, it was your Grandpap's."

I opened the plainly wrapped package. It was his old coffee thermos. The same one I remembered him hauling off to work every morning when they'd kept me as a kid.

"Oh Nana, thank you! You know I won't make it far without coffee!"

"That's your Grandpap in ya. And don't you forget, if you find you a home out there on the road, you at least gotta come back one more time to get that ring of his."

A part of me grew cold. What if Nana wasn't there when I got back.

Karma's 2nd birthday was even more of a spectacle than her first. She got treats, and toys, and a travel pillow - meant for her to sleep on. It wasn't five minutes after she opened the pillow that she had all its stuffing strown out across the floor. Mom brought out a Ribeye with two candles jammed into it and we all sang Happy Birthday while Karma nearly crawled out of her skin and the combined strength of mine and Peter's grasp waiting for her birthday steak.

After we turned her loose on the beef, I broke away from the party to get ready for the morning. I'd overloaded the Rodeo with everything I felt like we could possibly ever need and made Karma a spot in the back seat with my old bus trip blanket laid out for her. Feeling everything was in order, I went back inside and rejoined the party. Karma was posing for pictures for Mom.

"You guys can sleep in here tonight, wake us up when it's time."

"Thanks Mom. Tell Mom 'Thank you' Karma!"

Karma showered Mom with kisses and saved one for Dad as they made their way to bed. We kicked back on the couch and watched black-and-white reruns until we fell asleep.

When I woke, I made coffee and filled my Grandpap's thermos. The folks woke up to take Karma out for her last hometown yard patrol for a while and I ran through our preflight checklist. Peter called to wish us well, and an hour before the sun came up, we were heading down the road with the folks shrinking and waving in the rearview.

Karma had a whole living room in the back. We weren't even at the end of the folks' road before she made it clear that her accommodations were unacceptable. She climbed into the front seat and pushed all my notes and maps to the floor. Then, she sat up and faced forward with a straight back, eyes wide and bright, a smile on her face, looking at the asphalt ribbon unrolled before us. I'd stopped to let her get situated and to admire how game she was for our trip. Impatiently, she turned her brown eyes to mine and doubled her smile, making it clear she was ready to go now.

Chapter Five

I was determined to make a coast-to-coast run that summer. Our plan was to see Robert in Atlanta, then be on our first beach in Charleston, South Carolina by sunrise. After that, we would ride the east coast to Jacksonville for some more beach time. From there, we'd cross the Gulf Coast to New Orleans, and then shoot straight to the heart of Texas for Tom's place. After a break in Texas, we'd head north to see Jude and Mary in the mountains, then west, to see Ben on the Pacific.

We stopped at the gas station by our freeway exit to fill up and rearrange the Rodeo. I went inside to grab a quart of oil, snacks, and extra water. The tank was full by the time I got back, and Karma was in her seat calmly awaiting my return. I reset the gas pump with my free hand and reached for the door handle. Click. I pulled it again. Click... Panic. She had locked herself in and my keys were in the ignition. Karma looked at me with a blank expression and a dramatic blink. Then I remembered the jerky.

The windows were down enough to fit my fingers through with a piece of cheap jerky. My thinking was, she had hit the locks while squirming around and, if I was lucky, I could get her to hit unlock. As it turned out, patience was more important than luck. After a half hour of teasing her with bits of pressed beef at the window; she finally dropped her paw in just the right spot and unlocked the door. The station attendant, who had been watching the whole time with a locksmith's slim-jim in his hand, laughed and applauded. I gave Karma a big hug for saving the day and teaching me not to leave my keys in the ignition while my child was in the car.

She was fascinated with traffic. Any vehicle she could see people in was of great interest to her. In rural Georgia, we found something else of great interest to her - trailers of farm animals. We passed a truck of chickens and if we hadn't set a 2/3rds down rule on the window, I'm sure she'd have leapt out of the Rodeo at eighty miles per hour to chase down that truck.

We had time to kill and burned it at a rest stop, where she met her first travelers. Karma made friends with a dark-haired stranger while the stranger's husband picked his guitar in the shade and I talked with the Rodeo. Our beast of burden had no complaints about the longest journey it had seen since before Karma was born. Karma's stranger told me that I reminded her of the Fool.

"A Fool?" I asked.

"No, 'the' Fool, from the tarot cards! He travels around with a white dog that's always tryin' to stop him from wandering over cliffs."

She pulled the card from her deck to show me… she wasn't kidding.

"Do you want me to read your cards?" She asked.

I told her I already knew there was pain and torture in my future. She smiled and wished us well on our journey.

We had planned on a quick nap at Robert's, but once Karma met his pup, we were too amused by their bonding to sleep.

"I'm leaving for Boston next month; you guys should come up there when I get settled!"

"Absolutely man, you going to another apartment?"

"Not sure yet, I'm thinking about taking advantage of housing prices and maybe buying a place."

"I thought Pops was being paranoid when he sold his place a few years back but looks like he cashed out at just the right time!"

"Yeah, sixty some odd years on this earth will teach ya few things."

"I'm jealous of his generation, they seem like that have a place in this world. Sometimes I feel like we were born too late for one generation and too early for the next, like crops planted too late to harvest."

"Mark… You think entirely too much man."

In what seemed like a moment, the clock demanded that we leave. With promises to see each other again soon, we parted ways with our first hosts, Karma felt robbed by so short a meeting with her new sister. I was told Robert's dog felt the same.

We approached Charleston, sleep deprived, in the night. Several miles out, Karma rose from her slumber and started sniffing. I knew where we were, but it didn't occur to me she'd caught wind of the ocean until I smelled it myself. The smell was tainted with asphalt and concrete dust when we hit construction traffic downtown and all the lights and commotion got her in full rubber-neck mode. One woman with a traffic control sign and a seemingly perpetual scowl waved at her and smiled.

We got to the only beach I'd found that was dog friendly. It was just under an hour before sunrise, and we were right across the street from the ocean. I could see a lighthouse beacon lighting up the clouds, it was going to be an overcast sunrise, but we were right on time for it. I fixed us both a snack and got her bright red harness on her. After I filled my coffee mug from Grandpap's thermos, I hooked her onto her leash, and we made for the beach.

The sky was already showing hues of dawn, with a faint glow lighting the air. The tide was out, and the long glassy slope of its plain was showing. The Atlantic waters were just barely rolling up it with the waves. Karma explored the finer points of walking on loose sand for a bit, then we started moving toward the water. The first little splash of the waves startled her, but by the second or third wave she had figured it out and was chasing them as they rolled in and out.

It was so serene there, the lighthouse off in the distance, all the beachfront buildings dark, the sun coming up with the crisp smell of salt heavy on the damp air. As far as I could see in any direction, it was just me and Karma at the beach. She ran up to me and twirled around, then gave me a muffled bark, like she knew there was no one there to care if I let her off her leash.

I unlatched her and she took off, full sprint, down the shore. I saw my only companion on this journey shrinking onto the horizon and the sound I let out was nothing short of embarrassing. I'd gone so long without really caring about much of anything, and now this little brat had me shrieking in fear of losing her. She kept her stride but took the boost out of the steps. After a quick splash in the water, she came trotting back, overjoyed. She leapt toward me with a twirl and then licked the saltwater off my legs.

We sat on the sand and watched the sun come up. There was a window on the horizon, between the ocean and the clouds, a red sun came up through it. It was just hazy enough to look right at the sun without going blind. The narrowness of that window let you appreciate the motion of it, the motion of us, here on Earth, spinning around at the exact speed the sun was moving through that window.

As the clouds swallowed the red disc, our interest in it waned and we turned our attention back to the water. We hadn't bathed since we left, it was summer in the South, and I didn't see any beach showers in the area. I took a quick splash, then I dragged her into the deeper water to rinse off. Drenched, we paced up and down the beach to dry off. The clouds were burning off, but they were still thick, and the wet coastal breeze wasn't doing much to dry us.

The sun finally found a hole in the clouds after about an hour. I was adjusting to the light and thought I saw a person with two dogs in the distance. I rubbed my eyes and then, right in front of me, two greyhounds had appeared. The distant man let out a yell and sharp whistle. With blinding speed, the hounds flew back to their owner. I looked at Karma and said what I felt like we were both thinking,

"Did you see how fast they were?!"

Being polite southern folk, we made our way to the man and his hounds. He was skeptical, but his dogs and Karma seemed to feel like everything was okay, so he was cordial. We had a quick conversation and parted ways. As he left, he mentioned I would do well to move on,

"Not all the homeowners on this beach will be so friendly if you meet them." He said.

Enamored with the morning and not fully understanding what he'd told me, we continued up and down the shore to dry. It wasn't long before people started coming out on the beach and as advertised, they were the point-and-stare types.

I can't blame them; we were a mess. All the saltwater in my hair had matted it into clumps. Karma was soaked and sand covered from charging in and out of the surf. On top of that,

I had worn the most comfortable, and tattered, clothes I owned for the first leg of our trip. These buildings I'd thought were resorts or shops were, in fact, people's homes. Pacing the shore had disoriented me, but I remembered we were closer to the lighthouse when we entered the beach. We started making our way toward the flashing light.

Then I heard it. Two quick blares of a police siren behind us. A beach-tired SUV rolled up, and its window rolled down.

"Sir! Step over here Sir."

We complied. Karma started puppy eyeing the officer and put her paws on his step rails to get closer.

"Get her off the vehicle Sir, you will pay for scratches."

I didn't even bother to speak; I just took up the slack in her leash. He asked about my business, I explained our trip, he advised me dogs were only allowed on this beach for certain hours of certain days, and only with a permit.

"Today is not one of those days, Sir. Now, where is your permit?" He demanded.

I had seen nothing about a permit on the website and told him so. Completely unfazed, he began advising me that he could take my dog to the pound and charge me a $1000 fine, not counting the fees to get her out, and the three days wait to be sure she didn't have rabies symptoms.

I asked if we could just leave his state, and never again return so unprepared. He started to get out of the SUV and looked down at Karma. She waved her magic wand tail and gave him a big smile, then he sat back in his seat. I saw him throw her a little wink and a half grin behind his aviator shades and moustache before looking back at me and coldly stating.

"I think that would be a good idea, Sir. Carry on then."

We power walked back to the Rodeo. Then, in perfect abidance of every law, casually exited South Carolina, back into

Coastal Georgia.

That road was long, straight, hot, humid, and – like so many that year – mostly under construction. We'd lost a good bit of time lingering at the beach and with all the construction on that sweaty coastline. We had planned to leave Jacksonville before evening traffic but arrived on the wrong side of noon and decided to wait it out and drive into the night.

Jacksonville was a different world from Charleston. At a pit stop I had double checked all the regulations, to be sure we were moving into friendly territory this time. When we arrived at our second beach, we drove through a gap in the sand dunes to get into this bay-like area and parked right there on the sand. I had a chain in the back and hooked Karma to the trailer hitch. She calmly lounged in the sun on the white sands while I made us dinner.

We ate and enjoyed sitting still. We watched people come and go, families live their lives, a father teaching his daughter to surf. For all the commotion on that beach, it was a peaceful place – ships coming and going in the distance, people watching us watch them pass us by.

It seemed like there was a shift in Karma's attitude. From excitement and wonder to calm attention. Her curiosity was tempered. She wasn't as distracted by the people and their comings and goings. She just sat there, chained to the Rodeo with me, and soaked up the afternoon.

A few people passed by and gave her attention; when they went on their way, she went back to watching the waves. When we strolled the shore, she steadily followed the surf, in and out, so that it rinsed her paws every few yards. No more need to charge the crashing waves. It was like, in a matter of a few hundred miles, she adapted and it was just another day in the life of Karma.

The peace of that beach lulled us into a nap, but my alarm was merciless in the execution of its task. We loaded up, sand and all, into the Rodeo and made our way out of the bay. There was a sign for I-10 right at the exit. We made our turn, and in no time, the world was passing in a blur again. This time, we were going west to go west, to Texas, to a couch, and a real shower.

After rolling the windows down for air and triggering a sandstorm in the Rodeo, we pulled over at a truck stop carwash to vacuum our home. I made a check-in call to the folks, and they felt like I'd been up too long and needed to stop. I was gung-ho about making it to Texas before a nap. In a brilliant play of parental tact, they asked if I felt like Karma was safe with a driver in my condition, about 48 hours without any real sleep. I looked back at my pup; she was doing her best to get comfortable but struggling under the truck stop lights. After sitting up in the seat, she looked at me and let out this dramatic sigh before dropping her head down on the console and uttering a grunt of protest.

"You're right, we're an hour outside of Pensacola, we'll find someplace there to sleep."

"You drive, we'll make calls."

"Fine, I'll call from the last exit before town."

I felt ready for a little more space than the Rodeo could offer, and the hour to Pensacola seemed like days. My depth perception started to waver and, while I never got drowsy, I was zoning out. By the time we stopped to call home, I wasn't speaking all that well and, when we got to the motel, my condition was so bad I felt compelled to tell the receptionist half my life story to explain how I got there and that I had not been drinking. She tittered and giggled, glad for the amusement in the middle of the night. Karma stayed in the Rodeo, with her head on the console, motionless and snoring.

We got to our room and unloaded the basics. I pitched her in the tub and started the water to get the sand cleaned off her. I was filthy too, so I just jumped in and rinsed her and my dirty clothes under the shower. I don't think I even dried her off. I just turned her loose in the room and stripped down to shower myself up.

With fresh road clothes on, I flopped down on the bed next to Karma and woke up 30 hours later with no idea where I was. Karma was right there, still asleep. I composed myself and headed for the front desk to apologize for having only paid for one night and stayed two. The same girl that checked us in said that housekeeping had stopped by and Karma had greeted them at the door.

"Everything seemed to be okay, your dog hopped back on the bed with ya once she said hello to the housekeeper. They was pretty sure you was breathing and just pulled the curtain closed for ya and set out the do not disturb sign." She said.

I thanked her and asked how much I owed for the extra night; she said my parents had covered it. They'd called to check on us when I didn't answer my phone. I hadn't even looked at my phone.

I made my way back to give the folks a call, Karma was waiting at the door and leapt into the landscaping to answer nature's call. After checking in with the folks, everything in the Rodeo came out. We hadn't ridden our longest legs yet, and already we were uncomfortable. I rearranged everything so that Karma's seat laid flat and could be my bed at rest stops while she slept in the driver's seat. The console became a shared area, and I set up a little hand towel I brought (from the bathroom of the motel) to give it more cushion for us both. I had brought my tools in case we found an opportunity to make a dollar on the way, and in case the Rodeo broke - I compressed all that in the back. Anything we might need on the road went on the floorboard, under her reclined seat. I threw all my navigation paperwork out and notated the atlas Mom gave me with what I needed to know then stuffed it in a little pocket in the door.

We shuffled the CDs in the visor and did some research on the radio stations between there and Texas, then we decided to move the open window to the back, where Karma could sit and do her sniffing with me never having to worry about it, because that window didn't go all the way down.

After an afternoon of hustling, I was ready for bed again. I got my camera out and realized I'd spent this whole extra bit of money on a nice camera, and the only thing I'd used it for was pictures at the beach in South Carolina. We'd made at least six stops, and all I had was two pictures of Karma. I switched it on and got a shot of her buried in the blankets and one of myself in the mirror. I never cared much for pictures, especially not ones of me, but in that moment; I developed a love of photography, especially taking pictures of Karma. After a quick check of what was, and was not, in the Rodeo, I hopped in the bed and Karma stretched out on the other side of it like she knew it was back to the passenger seat tomorrow.

We woke up early enough for the free breakfast and got a full buffet sampler for myself, with eggs and bacon for Karma. On my way back to the room, this old timer passed me.

"What a gent, taking his lady breakfast!" He said.

I couldn't decide whether he was complimenting me or

picking on me, and wasn't sure what he'd think of the truth, so I just gave him a smile and a nod.

My eyes were bigger than my stomach and we ended up splitting my plate. Me and Karma, not the old-timer. We got our last bit of stuff together and left a thank you note for the staff, blaming Karma for the missing bathroom towel. I grabbed the camera and assorted front-seat stuff from the table and packed us up to get on the road again. When I turned back to the window, Karma had worked her way under the curtain and was staring at me. She had a look of pure despair on her face, like she thought I was going to leave her. In a long howl she cried:

"Don't leave me! Doooooon't leave me!!"

I hated to sustain her anxiety, but with the camera right there, I had to get a picture. When I opened the door, she ran straight for the Rodeo and jumped directly into her improved seat.

Chapter Six

After two days on the road and two in a motel, it seemed like no time, and we were cruising the French Quarter. Karma loved all the people she saw walking around, especially the ones in horse drawn carriages and the street performers. She sniffed and slobbered at the mist of voodoo spices that drifted through the window while the music from Bourbon Street filled the air and soundtracked what was, for me, a trip down memory lane. I wondered what I would have thought if someone had told me about what was waiting at home on my first trip down, or that I would be revisiting this place with a Pit-bull on a coast-to-coast road trip years later. I felt like I would've told them they'd had enough for one night.

We made a pit stop at a park and sat by a stream. Karma saw ducks for the first time; it was all I could do to keep her from lunging off in the water after them. They seemed accustomed to such behavior and paid her little mind. Other people were walking their own dogs, and it was funny to see the ones who feared us alter their paths to keep from crossing ours. On our way back to the Rodeo Karma spotted a rooster roaming around the grounds and tried to chase it down. The rooster eyed her coolly on her charge. Before she reached her target, she hit the end of her leash and slammed, face first, into the ground. I felt a little bad for her, but mostly laughed at how these birds could tell she was not a threat and the people in that park could not. The rooster scratched at the ground defiantly and Karma retreated to me, tail tucked, trying to shake the stars from her eyes as we made our way to the exit.

The thing you need to understand before you enter Texas is that for every mile you drive into that place, you are going to feel like you're driving two to get out.

Tom was living in a two-car garage that he'd converted into an apartment with a bathroom and galley kitchen up against the house. The rest of the space was just open, with two windows cut into the boarded-up garage door frames. His brother, Samuel, and his family lived in the main house. That evening we toasted to old friends rejoined, while Karma and her pops wrestled over a tennis ball on the floor.

I had gotten a handful of good pictures and posted them, then I accepted some friend requests and sent messages to Ben, Robert, and Jude - reporting our progress. Morning greeted us with an unexpected, exotic, and intoxicating fume of miso and charring fish set to the sound of children's laughter. For a moment I wasn't sure we were in Texas anymore.

Samuel had a wife and two toddlers, with another one the way. He was a martial arts teacher; his wife did fitness coaching and, together with her mother, they all tried to keep up with the kids. His mother-in-law lived in her own part of the house, called the kitchen. Her family was displaced from Japan by World War 2 and had drifted their way west from the island ever since, picking up all manner of mystical kitchen spells along the way, she seemed to always be exactly where she was needed and still never burn a dish. She had two little dogs, a Yorkie and another pup that looked like a rat with a perm, the dogs kept to themselves outside of mealtimes. Right there at that table, Karma and I somehow went from being freewheeling travelers to being a part of that family.

The kids instantly fell in love with Karma, and she shadowed every step they took. Her pops oversaw things from his spot on the sofa. Karma was always reluctant to follow me back to the apartment when it was time to wind down, torn between her loyalty to me and keeping an eye on those kids. The first time their mom noticed, she had a cuteness meltdown and started squealing.

"Awwwww, she loooooves them!!!"

Karma was born into a full house, but it was full of guests. This one was full of family. Everyone hustled around with a hive-mind, and Karma found her place in that flow far faster than I did. I'd never spent more than a few hours in a house with kids, but I eventually caught up with her, and them. We worked at the gym, we practiced martial arts, we ate, we slept, and we learned to live a life that was foreign to us. Life as a part of a 24/7 team.

Everything mirrored everything else there. Whether it was jiu-jitsu, dinner, or the kids, the same problem-solving mentality was always at play with them. Going for a knee-bar and getting caught in a heel-hook suddenly seemed no different from getting caught in traffic on the way to a show or dealing with one of the kids flipping out while we're all trying to get stuff done at the gym. There was never an issue, just a moment and a choice. Plan A gives way to plan B, you improvise a plan C and if you're calm, persistent, and lucky, you just might get out of whatever mess you're in.

One week's stay became a month. A month became almost two, and then we arrived at opening day of the gym. We celebrated on the patio, in the dry warmth of a Texas night. When our elation gave way to exhaustion, I realized how long we'd been there and how many miles we still had to go before we saw the cold grey waters of the southern Pacific. I broke a moment of natural silence to break the news.

"I think we'll probably be heading out this week man, we got a lot of miles left to go."

"Where's your next stop, bro?"

"Jude and Mary's up in Colorado, from there out west to see Ben."

"You still planning on tryin' to be back home for the holidays?"

"Yeah man, that's the plan. What've you got planned now that the work on the gym is done?'

"I don't know bro, just kinda taking it day by day. I like training, I'll prob'ly put some time into that."

"I noticed you don't spend as much time on the web, did that run its course for ya?"

"In a way, I guess. To be honest with ya, I just decided all that mess I was worrying over is just part of the plan."

"The plan?"

"Yeah, God's plan. I don't get it, but I guess I just realized I'm not supposed to."

"I've never really looked at the world that way, but I see the wisdom in it more as I get older." I conceded.

"I've been thinkin' I might go into some kinda ministering."

"Like a preacher?"

"I don't know, I can't see myself up in front of a bunch of people tellin' them how to live their lives, but one on one, with small groups… mainly just there to listen and talk, maybe. Maybe like a kung-fu monk or something! Whatcha gonna do when your journey is done?"

"Honestly, I haven't given it any thought. Before we got here, I was focused on finishing the journey. Once we got here. I found something unexpected in being a part of this team."

"It's not a team, it's a family, bro. And you and Karma are a part of it now."

"I appreciate that man. The miles ahead look lonelier than they did before we had this experience, but still a lot of different places to see."

Sam's mother-in-law, who we'd thought was sleeping in her chair, spoke up.

"I travel by land and sea from Japan, across Asia and Europe, sixty years, to right here, right now. Everywhere look different from far away. Everywhere has different buildings, different trees or rocks, but on a street, in a house, at a table, life is the same everywhere. It's not the memory you make for yourself, it's the memory you leave behind that's important."

She smiled and stretched her frail-looking, but terrifyingly strong, arm out toward the moonlit yard. Karma and both the kids had piled themselves up like pups in a litter and were asleep in the silver glow of the moonlight. We almost never left that place.

The morning we left, I went to round up Karma and walked into an emotional wrecking ball of a scene. The kids had huddled themselves around Karma, sobbing, and saying they loved her, and how they would miss her, and begging her to be careful. All the while, looking at me like I was an awful person for taking her away.

"So… here's a memory I wish I hadn't left."

Tom threw a hand of comfort on my shoulder. "That's love man, that's not a bad thing you're looking at."

"You know what I mean, I could've planned a little better and prepared them."

“You stayed ‘til the last possible day and you’re comin’ back someday, right?”

I don’t know if they heard us, but both boys were tugging on my arms for hugs. I squatted down to meet them at eye level.

“Be careful, we love you.” The younger whispered.

The older boy grabbed my shoulders and squared off with me, one inch from my face.

“If you can’t come back, it’s okay to just send Karma. We’ll take care of her.”

Then he gave me a hug.

We left and they went on about their day as a family. Somewhere on the lonely stretch of road that carried us across West Texas, I looked over at Karma, watching her world zoom by at eighty miles an hour.

“I’m proud of you out here, Karma. Everyone loves you and you just fit in everywhere."

She looked back, gave me a smile and a few happy pants, then she was back to watching the scrubby landscape vanish into the night.

At dawn, the sun rose on El Paso and Juarez. A great city split in half by a river. On one side, tall glass buildings, glistening in the sun. On the other side, by comparison, a crumbling ruin. I had been there before on my bus ride home. It struck me – as it had before - how powerful lines on a map can be. How different a life can be, depending on which side of that line you’re on. I wondered how different our lives would be when Karma and I finished drawing our line on the map. I was all too glad to turn a blind eye north and leave the conflict of that place behind us.

New Mexico was truly the land of enchantment. We passed from arid brown and tan landscapes into rolling grassy hills of yellow and green. In between, we visited the White Sands, a vast pile of snow-white gypsum bled out from the mountains around it. Karma romped and played in the blinding light of the midday sun reflecting off the dunes. We watched a group of kids sledding and snowboarding and I realized Karma had never seen snow. I wondered what else she hadn't seen that I just took for granted, how much of everyday life was still as awe-inspiring to her as this place was to me. It was incredible the way the landscape changed for just those few square miles and then reverted right back to high plains battling with the craggy foothills of the Rockies.

We passed through Albuquerque and onto Santa Fe, over the ruins of route 66, where a street fair was being held, people everywhere, selling things they'd made amidst aromas of native street foods dancing on the breeze. Karma looked with wonder on every face. Everyone waved, everyone smiled. It was so different from the cities we had seen, with its native vibe and limited vehicle traffic. The scene tempted me to stop, but daylight was fading, and our old friends were waiting.

Northbound, we crossed into Colorado with the sun setting over the mountains to my left. We were moving fast, but time seemed slow as the shadow of those purple peaks just barely wandered on the horizon. I'd never seen the Rockies before, and in the dusk, they didn't look that much different from the mountains in California. Hours later, when we started really approaching the Front Range, I realized how high their peaks had to be for us to see them from so far away.

Karma slept that last stretch of our road. Despite not being able to speak, she really was great company when she was awake. After our stay in Texas, it got lonely in the Rodeo when she slept. When we finally arrived at Jude and Mary's, I was exhausted. Jude met us in the driveway and showed us inside. Mary and the boys were waiting on the couch, all thrilled to see familiar faces at last.

We sat up for a bit, the boys gave Karma a tour and Jude ran them through their tricks. We talked about where we'd been and what we'd seen, but within an hour, I was out of gas. They gave us the couch and retired to their room. Karma hopped up beside me and stretched out between me and the back of the couch. Before I drifted off to sleep, it hit me that there was just one more couch to crash on, one more stretch of road before we reached our goal. The miles behind us had gone by so fast… I fell asleep thinking about what Tom had asked – what will we do when all this is done? What's to become of us when we run out of road, and turn our wagon back home?

I woke up the next morning and took Karma outside. Over to the West was the most amazing sight so far. Rising, high above the urban sprawl, dwarfing the largest and tallest buildings in the city, Pike's Peak looked down on this bustling town of Colorado Springs. Even in August, there was snow on top. I'd never seen anything so massive, so dominant in the sky. It blew my mind that right in their back yard was such an impressive sight, such a natural wonder, but no one around us seemed to pay any mind.

"You get used to it." Jude shrugged.

"I don't see how man, that's the biggest thing I've ever seen!"

"Life, dude. Life is happening down here on the ground. That's just a distraction when you're sitting in traffic at 5 o'clock on a Wednesday afternoon. You've gotta see Garden of the Gods while you're here, I still haven't gotten used to that. One thing though, no pups."

Helping Tom at the gym was the only time I'd left Karma's side on this trip. Even then, I'd left her in the care of a whole family. I cringed at leaving her alone in her cage, but Mary assured me the boys would keep her company. Staring up, in awe, at that mountain's round peak, I figured the Garden must be something to see.

On our way to the Garden, we never escaped the Peak, everywhere we went it was looking down, calling me to see the world through its eyes.

"Have you guys ever climbed the mountain?"

"We drove up when we first moved, it a gorgeous view." Mary said.

"You can drive up there?!?"

"Yeah dude, don't you remember it from racing games?" Jude said. "You can take that same road up."

Right there, I decided. We were going to the top of that mountain.

We came to Garden of the Gods, in all its splendor. Red and brown and yellow stone all carved by dead rivers and the wind into sculptures for our imaginations to name. It reminded me of the White Sands and how different a place can be from the places that surround it. It was like a hallowed space where the worries of 9 to 5 life were unable to go. We walked that place for hours, climbed on little boulders, watched the fire department rescue a group of college kids who had climbed up Kissing Camels with no rope, leaving themselves no way to come back down.

I'm ashamed to say that being in that strange place with such old friends, I forgot where I was, even when I was. I forgot Karma was locked in a cage half an hour away. To my relief, Karma seemed happier for the break. I promised her tomorrow, we'd go on an outing of our own, and look down on the world from 14,000 feet.

At the base of the mountain, it became clear I had forgotten to ask the most important member of our travelling tribe what it thought… the Rodeo. As we started the slow climb, stuck in line, waiting for our turn to drive up that road, the Rodeo began to complain, getting hotter with each moment that passed. I looked over at Karma, maximally excited, and back at the Rodeo's temperature, critically heated. I was determined to get up there, but not at this cost. Within 15 minutes of being in line, I sounded the retreat. I apologized to Karma, and the Rodeo, for our whole trip back to Jude's.

Since we'd left home, it was the first defeat we had suffered, and it brought the tide of reality crashing back to the shores of our wanderlust dream. Still, I couldn't let it go, and I remembered what I'd learned in Texas. I had to get up there, I needed a Plan B.

It was all I thought about after pushing the Rodeo to its limit. I spent that night looking at trails and pictures. I inspected the worn-in army boots Jude had given me when his uncle died; they had become my primary footwear on this journey and seemed up to the task. Before we all crashed for the night, I asked if they would mind if I left Karma with them for a day. I was going to the top of that mountain, even if I had to do it on foot.

"You're going on foot?!" Jude asked.

"I don't see another way."

"Not being a madman is the other way, dude! There's no air up there, it's like breathin' nothing. Plus, I'm pretty sure you rode a ski lift to the only mountain tops you ever saw. Have you ever even hiked?"

"Not really… But I never had a Karma or took a cross country road trip and that's all turned out okay so far."

He cackled like a mad villain.

"So far!! Pushing your luck is what got you here, dude – the good and the BAD parts of that story. Do what you gotta do, but if you're not back in a day, we're calling mountain rescue and if a bear eats you alive, we're keepin' Karma!"

For over six hours I fought rocks and roots, branches and grass made slick by the dew. The switchbacks drove me insane, walking a hundred feet to climb two. I was trekking up the west side and when the sun finally came over the ridge, it was blinding. The ground was covered in diamonds, little pockets of snow lingered in holes that have never seen the light. The grass grew thinner, the trees grew shorter and in a straight line across my view, it all just turned to rock. Then it was barren stone for what seemed like miles. There was no oxygen in the gasps of air my sea-level lungs struggled to take, only the smell of evergreens. It felt like drowning. I came to a large rock wall with a gap in it – and right through that door, I finally saw the Peak.

A few steps, rest, a few more, rest. When I came to the ridge that looked down on the road, the same road that had turned us back the day before, I stopped. Cars zigged and zagged up the asphalt and where I thought I would feel envy, I just felt sorry for them all. They could breathe, but all they'd seen was concrete and painted lines on their journey.

A few steps, rest, a few more… Then, finally, I reached the base of the peak. It was a pile of house-sized pink granite boulders, stacked five hundred feet high. Adrenaline kicked in and I scrambled through the maze. Out of breath, with shaking legs, and trembling hands I climbed. Then, I saw it. Over the top of the last rock was… a donut shop.

It was an old weather station converted into a welcome center. They sold mile-high donuts, coffee, and souvenirs. I was almost disappointed that all my struggle had led me to a tourist trap, but then, I smelled the warm beckoning of donuts and coffee in the thin mountain air.

I ordered three donuts and a large coffee to regain my strength. Mile-high donuts are very dry, but the view was spectacular, looking out over the curvature of the earth, the sprawling city to one side, and in all other directions, just mountains and valleys and lakes, as far as the eye could see. From that Olympian vista, my eyes kept scanning the city, trying to figure out where Jude and Mary's house was, to look down on where Karma was. With one last look around the summit, and a camera battery's worth of pictures, I left that strange and beautiful place.

I didn't climb down so much as fall, slide, and crawl. I had read that coming down was the hard part. It seemed odd because gravity was helping you – but gravity is not your friend. My legs had not taken that many steps in a day, ever! By the time I got back to the Rodeo, I was cut, bruised, exhausted, and convinced that a bear had been stalking me through the woods.

Back at Jude's, they were all asleep. He woke up to check on me and asked if I'd made it all the way up. I gave him a shaky thumbs up and he just shook his head in disbelief. I broke it to Karma I couldn't share the couch and I needed her to spend a night in the cage.

"Daddy is broken sweetheart."

As soon as I could walk, it was time to say goodbye to our

friends with hugs, tail sniffs, and licks; then we pointed our wagon west for the final leg of our trip.

Chapter Seven

We passed through Utah in the night and stopped in the literal middle of nowhere to stretch my still aching legs. The one streetlight at that rest stop was the only visible light for as far as I could see. Karma was uneasy, and I even felt like the only thing that place was missing was a sign that read, "Please wait here for the next available kidnapper."

There was a meteor shower that night and with no light pollution, it was raining fire. I felt a cosmic humility looking at how beautiful it was and thinking about how if just one of those things was a little bit too big, we all go the way of the dinosaurs. Everything that ever happened on this rock could be erased from the record in a flash. Forever.

After a while, under the technicolor streaks of space debris crashing into Earth, I was less concerned about ending up on a true crime special and took my spot in the Rodeo with Karma.

We awoke surprisingly refreshed. Still not a soul in sight, nor any sign that one had been our way. We were completely alone out there. Looking out across the horizon, I could see the Utah landscape was gorgeous and regretted driving all that way in the dark. Then, it occurred to me that the mountains are lasting and would be there, while the falling of the night sky was fleeting and had to be seen in its own time; regret gave way to grateful reflection.

Soon enough, I remembered we were in a hurry and the world was zipping by our windows again. We ran into traffic in a huge gorge on the western side of the state, and slowly crept through the winding chasm. We were following the course of an ancient waterway that hadn't survived into our time, a place where dinosaurs had come to drink once. It was claustrophobic compared to the landscapes we'd travelled, and we were both glad to get out of that hole and into the vast open of the Great Basin.

I was driving us to south Cali by way of Vegas. In all the history of travel perhaps the worst decision one could make in the United States is trying to pass through Las Vegas in the middle of the day. It was hot, it was loud, there were people everywhere, and they were all stumbling through the streets. Even Karma seemed less interested in the goings-on and more interested in moving along from there, then we met the Mojave.

The Rodeo's AC was never great, and it had run non-stop through Vegas. In the desert heat of the Mojave, running it was a lost cause. There were no gas stations for something like two hundred miles, and as it seemed futile, I just turned off the air and rolled down the windows. It was like driving through an oven with a hair dryer blowing in your face. Karma was laying on her back with her arms out like she was on a cross, her tongue hanging into the floorboard, and she was looking at me with contempt.

"Not what you signed up for Karma?"

We had gallons of water, so I pulled over somewhere between Baker and Barstow to douse us both. We were bone dry before we could even get back to the Rodeo and I think I smelled her paws cooking on the pavement. When we finally got out of there, we were hours from our destination. Not months, or weeks, or even days. It was about to happen. We had set out to make a coast-to-coast road trip, now we had only a handful of miles and mountain passes between us and the sea.

Racing the sun to the coast, we sped. I hadn't planned to get there at sunset, but the sun's descent toward the water hiding behind that last ridge seemed perfectly timed to our arrival. All by chance. I had this one spot I wanted to go to and couldn't remember how to get there. With no time to figure it out, I opted to just get to the Pacific Coast Highway.

Climbing up the last ridge, the one that looked out over the coast, Karma perked up. I knew from the top of that hill we would be able to see the water. She smelled it already and after all the dry heat of the day's journey, we were both imagining charging off into that cold murky water of the Pacific.

She ran to her open window and was wagging her tail so fast that it felt, pleasantly, like a fan running behind me. I hadn't seen that ocean in years. The Pacific swallows you up when you see it. It doesn't look much different in pictures, but there's something out there in all that emptiness, something in its enormity that forces you to feel small.

In the few miles left to the shore, I drove all the way back to South Carolina in my mind. I remembered the everyday actions of my passenger more than anything. Karma in her seat, the Rodeo, the road, and the places we'd been – all of it came back at once. When walked out the folk's front door to begin this trip, Karma had no idea what we were about to do. Now, she knew exactly what we were going to do. We stopped at the first beachside pull-off we found and I harnessed her up and latched her onto her retractable leash. With four steps, we were back on a beach.

The west coast beaches weren't like the groomed beaches she'd seen. Rocky and tide strewn, full of life and places for it to hide, they were natural. She took her time exploring. The Pacific was excited to see us and sent a splash of foam to our feet. Karma returned to her memory of the Atlantic and charged the surf. She met a wall of water, twice as tall as her and was blown off her feet into the swell. She rolled and tumbled halfway back to my feet in the surf. Hacking and coughing, shaking and snorting, she hobbled the few steps back to me and sat facing the ocean respectfully.

"That happen my first time too sweetheart."

The sun hid its retreat from the sky behind a veil of clouds and memories of our trip washed up with every wave. Karma was laying in the sand with her head on my lap, the lullaby of the tide singing her to sleep. I felt the victory of the moment, but it was pale in comparison to my gratitude for the journey and being able to share it with this little mutt that almost didn't make it. All the mountains we sat out to climb, the sights we'd sat out to see, even mighty Pikes Peak seemed small here at the end of America.

We settled into Ben's place later that night. It was a mission style ranch. The house had a clay tile roof and a stonework courtyard with a big fire pit in the middle of the structure. He had bought it at auction, its former owner was another casualty of the housing meltdown. Ben fell in love with a girl and moved her and her kid both in.

His ranch smelled like orange blossoms and pine needles unless the wind came up from the cattle ranch below. His girlfriend's kid said it smelled like "dairy air" when that happened. The pastures were dry and brown but strown across the fields bloomed these little shoots of bright turquoise blues and lemon yellows that, small as they were, gave a bright and vibrant feeling to the near barren landscape. His driveway was lined with Torrey Pines that shaded the house and it's courtyard from the evening sun. Off in the valley we could hear cattle mooing on a farm. It was immediately deemed the calmest place we'd stayed on that trip.

The trip through the desert had left me feeling like a baked good and the sand from the beach was like a cinnamon sugar coating. Everything itched and my left arm was sun-scorched. I don't know if it was all that filth or the gravity of being there at the end of the road, but the shower I had that night was like a baptism that somehow diminished everything that had come before and gave weight to everything that could, maybe, come after.

We spent that first week revisiting my old haunts and taking Karma to some parks and beaches I remembered. Out in Valley Center, we finally sat on a cliff looking down on the world from on high together. She sat and scanned the vista, almost confused and decidedly aware of what happened if she slipped off the ledge.

We tried to catch up with some old friend while we were there, but most had moved beyond our reach. I had reluctantly left my snowboard and surfboard out there when I fled back home on the bus and was shocked to find my friend in L.A. still had them. I couldn't resist. Full as the Rodeo was, I would make room for a six-foot surfboard I nearly drowned on and a five-foot, razor edged, snowboard I'd bought when I was seventeen to learn snowboarding with Jude.

We spent most nights around the fire, Ben and his girlfriend listened to stories of our adventure, while Karma played with her daughter. They chased each other around the edge of the light, barking and giggling, until Karma caught her and licked her to death.

"Where you guys headed next, Cuz?" Ben asked.

"I promised Nana I'd be home for Thanksgiving, and I promised Tom's people I'd stop by on my way, so looks like Texas first, then back to where we started."

"Any plans for after the holiday? Y'all are welcome to come back out here and chill, there's plenty of room."

"Robert is moving north for work, he invited us up there in the spring. The Rodeo needs some TLC, so I'm thinkin' we'll winter at home, then make our way north."

"You tryin' to get through the lower forty-eight with your pup?"

For a moment I didn't know the answer to that question.

"…I think that's the plan man, we're gonna hit all of New England while we're up there, then figure out some roundabout trip through the north country in the summer maybe." I finally replied.

It didn't feel the same as when I had told people we were going to run coast to coast, something had changed. It was good to be around family again, but it got me thinking more about where I came from than where I was.

"If I don't make it home for the holidays, take Nana a hug for me?

"For sure! Hey, I never even congratulated you! How does it feel to be special ops?"

"I could tell ya, but then I'd have to kill ya!"

That drew a slap to his arm from his girlfriend.

"Nah Cuz, I'm proud, more than proud. I feel like this is where I belong."

This comment drew his girlfriend's hand into his and

earned him a kiss on the cheek.

We gave a day to the beach near the end of our stay. I let his girlfriend and her kid walk Karma up and down the sand while me and Ben called Nana up. For all the words exchanged in that conversation, it was the answer to her last question that brought her the most joy.

"Where's Karma off to next?!" she asked.

"Nana, Karma's comin' home."

Her response was just a happy noise.

Me and Karma drove up the Pacific Coast Highway to Los Angeles for my boards before heading home. After collecting my souvenirs, we had to go south a bit before going east. Karma never took her eyes off the ocean or brought her nose in from that window. Her ears flapped like pigtails in the warm air of that afternoon, and she took in breath after deep breath of the salty air and exhaust fumes until we turned onto I-10 and watched the city swallow the sea in our rearview mirrors.

It was the same road I had taken home from California when I abandoned it before. We crossed Joshua Tree and the Colorado River in the night and somewhere in the desert of Arizona, we stopped to watch the sunrise paint the lands red. By noon, it was too hot for both of us and I pulled off at a huge truck stop.

I told Karma to stay and went inside to stand in front of a cooler with the door open. On my way, I realized this was the same stop where the blanket had come from, the one that Karma had made her own through all this trip. I turned to look, and two Greyhounds were parked off to the side, just like mine had been when I took my ride home. I wondered if there were any young bucks on a bus heading home with their tails tucked and hoped they would be so fortunate as to find their own Karma somewhere down the road if so. After frosting myself in the walk-in cooler, I walked memory lane to the Rodeo.

Then, I learned that true love is when your dog leaves a steaming pile in your car, and you get mad at yourself for not putting her needs first. To her credit, she was surrounded by fabric seats and carpeted floors. Only the console between us was vinyl, covered in a stolen hotel hand towel. How she did it I will never know, but she dropped that bomb right on the center of it, in a perfect undisturbed pile. Her eyes were full of shame. I assured her that it was my fault and helped her out into the warm breeze. After I chained her to the back of the Rodeo, where signs and awnings shaded the grassless rocky earth. I cleaned up the mess I'd made in the merciless Arizona sun.

Nothing had changed much back in Texas. Sam's wife was further along, the Gym was a little busier, the Kids were a little rowdier, but overall, it was just as we had left it, only it didn't feel the same. They welcomed us to stay for as long as we wanted to stay, but after two nights with our Texas family, I started thinking about getting back to our own. For maybe the first time since we'd left home, Katherine crossed my mind.

We decided to check more states off our map on the way home. Our roundabout road took us through the Midwest in late fall and the further north we went the thicker the clouds became. As the sun set, the gathering storm started to churn. The rain began in the fading light of dusk. When the thunder and lightning came, Karma gave me an uneasy look, but never abandoned her post as co-pilot. The wind whipped us from lane to lane and the rain blew sideways. I wondered if a tornado was about to rip us off the road, out into the night and it was the first time on the whole trip I was afraid we might never make it home again. It finally passed, but when we made our eastern turn, it loomed out on the horizon ahead of us, on its way to unleash that fury on our family. That made me more nervous than driving in it.

We finally pulled off the freeway and into the same gas station where our adventure had begun. After being out west, it struck me how green the landscape was at home, how much life there was here compared to some places out there. I asked the clerks about the storm, and they said there was heavy wind and rain, but no major damage. Relieved, I bought a stick of jerky and took it back to Karma. She was sitting in her seat, smiling, with thousands of miles and seventeen states under her collar. She'd only had one accident and caused no property damage or personal injury claims. I gave her a kiss and fed her a treat before firing our road-grimed Rodeo up and putting it in gear.

"Let's get you home Sweetheart."

Chapter Eight

My folks were ecstatic to have their baby back home – Karma, not me. We pulled into their driveway and they charged out clapping and cheering. Karma jumped and twirled and licked them both. They showered her with hugs, kisses, and praise.

"We're so proud of you! You were so pretty on the beach, and so good with all the kids! Tell us all about your new friends."

Karma ate up every word. While I was leaning on the Rodeo, watching all this go down, I noticed something about my little girl. She'd enjoyed everywhere we went, loved everyone we'd met, marveled at every sight we'd seen, but in all those miles, I never saw her as excited and happy as she was right then.

After they wore each other out, the folks came to check on me. I was unloading our stuff to make the Rodeo a little more practical for local travel. They gave me hugs and said they were proud and caught me up on what little had happened since we left town. When they asked about my plans, I told them we'd camp in the garage, probably couch surf a bit, and that I was going to sign back up at the factory to refill our accounts, then somewhere in the spring, head up north.

From there we went to Peter's. Things hadn't changed much. It was a little bit cleaner, and the amplifiers weren't up quite so loud. One of Peter's friends had my old room and there was a fresh batch of kittens running around. They were all Russian blue, a few with tails a few with without. Every one of them was curious about Karma. She gave each one a sniff and a lick to welcome them to the world.

We spent that night on the couch, telling our tales and answering questions about pictures I'd posted. When it was finally just me and Peter, all he wanted to hear about was the mountain and Ben's ranch.

"That climb just about killed me man, hardest physical thing I've ever done, I literally fell all the way back down to the Rodeo."

"What about Ben's place? That looked like something out of a western."

"It was awesome, lots of space but a little run down. I guess the owner had abandoned it and Ben got it for a song at a foreclosure sale."

"Is he gonna work the land?"

"He wants to keep the orange trees but wasn't planning on bringin' cattle back or anything. He's hoping the markets will pick back up and he can cut lots off to sell to the cattle ranchs in the valley below him."

I could see Peter's wheels were turning but we abandoned our conversation when I went to check on Karma. I found her lying on her side with a small army of kittens trying, vainly, to have dinner.

"Pete! Come look at this mutt!"

We filled his house with howls of laughter.

"That's not how that works sweetheart! Those aren't your babies." Peter informed her.

The kittens were all lined up at Karma's dinner table, but no matter how much they clawed and bit, they couldn't get a drop of milk. Karma never moved a muscle. She just laid there and let them try. We spent most of our time at Peter's and every time we walked through the door, she went straight for 'her' litter and laid over on her side.

To everyone's surprise, she started making milk. Unsure what to do, we called up Doc.

"It's not ideal, but it shouldn't hurt either of them."

With that, we let it be, and Karma became Nubs' favorite thing in the world. As soon as she heard Karma's claw clacking on the linoleum floor, she would abandon her motherly post for a safe spot on the counter and hand her babies over to the nurse.

We made regular trips to Nana's too. The first few visits were just like everywhere else, telling our tales, answering questions, and talking about our next trip. I don't know whether it had been that way, or if I just noticed it then, but the silver threads in Nana's hair seemed like they were starting to outnumber the darker ones. When we stopped by to see her around Halloween, she didn't ask about our trip.

"So, do I owe you a ring Sweetpea?"

"Jury's still out on that Nana, you can keep it for now."

"Well, you just let me know when the verdict is in."

"I surely will Nana. Are you excited about Thanksgiving?"

"Of course!! I love havin' my family 'round the table more than anything. I'm glad you brought that up, we're gonna have a few empty chairs and I was wonderin' if you wanted to bring a guest like we talked about last year?"

"A guest?"

"Yeeeesss, your little girl has been everywhere with you now, it's only right she come to eat with her family."

"You wanted me to bring Karma to play with Grace! I'm

sorry Nana, I totally forgot about that!"

"She's family too, she should be in here with us. It looks like she's got better manners than Gracie, so we'll fix her plate, and she can help keep an eye on the great-grandkids for me."

Poor Grace always got parked in the garage for Thanksgiving, I felt like it wasn't fair, but I could also tell Nana wasn't taking no for an answer. Karma introduced herself to every aunt, uncle, cousin, and child in attendance. We made her a little plate of turkey and ham and put her by the kid's table. It didn't last long, then she was making her rounds to see which members of her extended family would pass her scraps. The year before had been all debates and opinions, this year was all Karma. Everyone raved about her and asked about our trip. Not a word was spoken about finances, football, business, or politics.

We were the first to leave, Karma's litter was going to find homes the next day and I wanted her to have one more night pretending to be a mommy before they went. Nana walked us out.

"Thank you so much for bringin' her, that was the best meal we've had in a long time!"

"Thank you for havin' us! We had a good time, didn't we Karma?"

Karma gave a little twirl of agreement and licked her Nana's hand. Nana bent down as best she could and gave Karma a kiss on her head. She waved us the whole way down the drive, and shouted,

"I love you two babies, come back anytime!"

The door to Peter's wasn't even open before Karma was barreling inside. Nubs had cut the litter off milk but still made her way to the counter to keep an eye on them with Karma. There was a wicked look in her eyes while she watched Karma wince at their pin-sharp teeth as they ate. I kicked back on the couch and Peter went back to his room. When every kitten's belly was full, Karma joined me on the couch but kept her head hanging off, eyes fixed on her litter until I fell asleep.

Peter got up to take them away, and she was a wreck. She whimpered and whined, every time he put one in the box, she tried to get them back out onto the floor. I finally had to load her up and take her to see the folks. She was pitiful, even there. Mom and Dad talked to her, but she didn't want to play. She just laid on the floor with sad brown eyes cast down and about every few breaths let out a faint grieving sound. She wasn't right for weeks; Peter and I came back from seeing a mind-blowing 3D movie that had just come out and found Karma laying and whining where the kitten had been. It broke our hearts. I was starting to wonder if even Christmas was going to cheer her up, but as soon as she saw the lights on the tree and all the shiny presents wrapped underneath, she was back to herself, ready to rip and tear and shred all the paper, cardboard, and bows.

At the New Year's party, she was a social butterfly with every guest at Peter's, but she kept sniffing around, I assumed for the kittens. When the party wound down, she found a spot on the floor, curled up in a ball, and gave a little sigh. I told her I was sorry her babies were gone, but that she had been a good mama. About that time, Nubs pranced over. Karma gave her a lick and Nubs rubbed her head against Karma's face, they curled up together and slept until the first light of that new year.

I started back at the factory at the end of that week, still living in the folks garage. Robert called asking if we could postpone my visit until Fall. He'd bought a cabin in the woods of New Hampshire and was wanting to focus on fixing it up. I offered to come help, but he said he wanted to do it himself.

"Just need a project man, city life is getting to me." He'd said.

We agreed to make it happen and my life again became a process of planning my next journey.

Winter and spring were work. Working at the factory, working on the Rodeo, working on the plan for visiting the rest of the lower forty-eight. I fought that engine all winter long. I stripped the whole front off and had all its parts in little plastic bags all over the place. Karma was convinced I was withholding food from her and incessantly sniffed at the Rodeo's guts. She seemed just as happy as anywhere in that situation, even with my grumpy self.

Without much fanfare, one day I reached the point in my work on the Rodeo that it was time to fix the problem and start putting the pieces back together. When I got down to the water pump, the thing killing it, I was amazed at how simple of a part it was, all I'd done was figure out what could be wrong and started pulling parts until I got to that, I never looked into the part and hadn't bought a new one because I knew I'd need a bunch of gaskets and stuff and just wanted to get it all at once. It's a little fluid turbine and an aluminum casing and it moves oil and water and if it fails somewhere in that simple operation, it probably kills your engine, like a heart. It got me thinking that maybe somewhere down in the middle of this life-engine called a mind, there something like a water pump and mine might be busted. I'd struggled with being grounded, but Karma's life seemed completely unperturbed. We had visitors, the parents spoiled her rotten and she never missed a beat.

When it was done, the motor was back in one piece at least.

I fired up the engine with ice in my veins and she sounded rough at first, like gravel or an old person groaning as they got out of chair. But as her blood got flowing, she sounded like my old Rodeo again. A little smoke out of the back cleared up on our test drive and after 3 trips around the block I brought her into port and let her idle. Oil looked good; water looked good. 15 minutes, looks good, 30 good, an hour and we're about out of gas, but looks gut, shut her down. We were back on the road.

I was on the overnight shift and Karma was alone in the garage while the folks were trying to sleep. Peter and I had one day different in our schedules, so I rode with him four nights a week and rodeoed on the fifth. The parents reported on what Karma did from the moment I left until she heard me pull back in,

"She just GRIEVES!" Mom said.

"I'm sorry…"

"No, it's okay, we feel sorry for her!"

"Oh… well if she's keepin' you up, just yell 'bad karma' at her, she hates that."

"She is a good Karma! We are not going to do that!"

One night, working by myself, on my last break, I got back to my phone with five missed calls – all my folks, all back-to-back. Nana was my first thought and I rushed to call them back. Dad answered.

"Is antifreeze toxic to dogs?!"

Mom was in the background behind him, wailing. They'd gone out to give Karma a break and found her standing over a jug of antifreeze spilled on the floor. Panic gripped me.

"I'm pretty sure it is, let me call you back."

I called our vet's emergency line, thankfully Doc answered.

"I think Karma has gotten into antifreeze, I'm not sure if

it's the non-toxic kind or what."

"Do you know how long ago? Do you have the bottle?"

"Not really, I'm 6 hours into a 8-hour shift, so no more than 6 hours…"

"If it has been in her system for 6 hours, then there isn't much we're going to be able to do for her. You should induce vomiting."

"Can I bring her in?"

He firmly answered, "You probably should."

I hung up the phone and called the folks to walk them through vomit induction, then ran back inside to ask if I could leave early for this emergency. Before I could get a word out, my supervisor caught me.

"There you are! Hey, so I know it's last minute, but we're doin' mandatory overtime today, we need you to stay two extra hours." He said with a smug grin.

I couldn't count the times he'd said that since I started there. Usually, I looked at it like extra money in my pocket, but that day it was time out of my life I wasn't willing to give up.

"Mandatory?"

"Yep! Time and a half!"

"Yeah, I quit."

Mom called me on my way home.

"We called and agreed to pay the afterhours fee, Doc says he can run some tests to be sure if she did or didn't drink it."

"I'm on my way there, thank you…"

I drove to the clinic, terrified I was going to show up to a dead Karma. Instead, I found my folks, Doc, and Karma walking around, looking relieved. Doc spoke first,

"I think she's okay, she doesn't have any symptoms and her

tests came back clean, looks like she spilled it but didn't drink enough to hurt her."

Before I could utter a word of thanks or comment on Karma's survival skills, Mom interjected.

"And she's moving inside!"

We moved into the guest room at my folks' that day. Karma took to it better than I did. After so many years out from under their roof and so many miles spent out on the road, I imagined I felt like Karma did when she was locked in her cage. I found work running rescue transports at Peter's old shelter, moving pups to places with more need and better systems for taking care of the poor orphans.

When the day of my first transport came, I left just like it was another day at work. A quick run up to Chicago and I was back. When Karma met me at the door, she had a look of suspicion as she sniffed up and down my pants. When I knelt for a kiss, she denied me, sniffing my shirt and collar, then snorting in disgust. I could see it in her eyes. She knew I'd been travelling without her and to make it worse, I'd been with other dogs.

When my birthday came around, Peter showed up just as Dad finished the main course. Nothing was said but I could tell something was up, even Karma seemed, I don't know… off.

"We all went in together and got you and Karma something. Karma this is for you too, but we are sorry – we can't let you open it sweetie."

Peter went out to his truck and came back with a book-sized box. Now beyond curious what had gotten the whole family to conspire together and what Karma couldn't open, I quickly tore it open.

"Holy cow! A tablet! Nicely done family! Look at this Karma, no more lugging an oversized laptop around in the Rodeo with us!"

I had complained about the hassle of lugging around my twenty-pound gaming laptop for the sole purpose of getting pictures off my camera and onto the web. Tablets were a brand new thing then and it was a near-miracle they'd been able to get one.

Karma's expression was pure disappointment, I could feel her saying,

'I can't believe you didn't let me open that, it's a big smartphone!'

"Don't worry sweetheart, your birthday is comin' up soon!"

Then, just like that, Karma was 3. We all came together to celebrate our girl. She tore through her birthday steak and all her presents with skill and grace, strowing trash clear from the kitchen into the living room, down the hall and into every open room.

Peter lingered around that night; I could tell something was on his mind. I found him on the patio after Karma had worn herself out and retired to the couch with Dad.

"What's on your mind brother?"

"I'm just flabbergasted they let Karma move inside."

"Same! But seriously, I can see your wheels turning. What's up?"

"Goals, brother, goals…"

"Setting your sights on something or just tryin' to zero in?"

"There's nothin' I really wanna do that amounts to a living. I liked work at the rescue because I was outside, workin' with life, but the factory jobs I've been doin' since have about killed me."

"I feel that man. I used to think about tryin' to go into game design, but that tour of duty in corporate technology burned that dream out. It's all so much office politics and social engineering. Now, I couldn't name a single job I can see myself wanting to do. You thinkin' about going back to the shelter?"

"Nah man, I'm thinkin' about that picture you took at Ben's, the one looking down from the hill over that ranch – I'm thinkin' that looks like a pretty good life for me."

"I can see you doin' that, Pa was a rancher, and Grandpap always kept that garden and chickens. It's in the blood."

"I've been talking to people; I found an old timer out in the county who's looking for a hand. It's a big pay cut, but he said he'd teach me about running a farm, help me get my bearings in that world."

"Can't beat a good mentor."

"I'm thinkin' about asking if the folks will clear out that storage room and let me move back here once my lease is up."

"A chance for Liz to have both her boys under one roof? I guarantee she's taking that deal."

"But there's the cats."

"Cat's, plural?"

"Oh yeah… Nubs is carrying again."

"Oh, for the love man, seriously?!"

"I'm gonna get her fixed this time for real, I wanna keep one of her runts, just for posterity."

"Might I suggest keepin' a boy?"

Peter chuckled as that was exactly his plan.

"Of course, it'll be my luck it's a litter of girls." He added.

"That worked out well for me so far."

"Indeed, it did brother, indeed it did. You give any thought to what you'll do when your road days are done?"

"I've thought a lot about what I want, tried to think about what I need, haven't given much thought to what I'll do though. It's like you said, nothin' really seems like my thing out there."

"I envy Ben. Dude knows who he is and what he needs to do."

"Same. All I know for sure right now is that I'm happier with Karma around and she is happier around here, so I'm not sure what the different desires that have come and gone in my life are worth compared to that."

"You know she'll follow you anywhere."

"Facts. I just don't know how I'd feel if something happened out there and she never got to see her family again."

I remembered that storm we drove through so clearly when I said that, remembered worrying about Nana, and thought about how nothing we'd seen or done really would have been as spectacular if we hadn't done it together. Peter and I whittled away what was left of our energy looking at the stars, trying to decide which ones to shoot for.

In autumn, I got the call. I'd spent all summer playing with my tablet, tuning up the Rodeo, and carrying homeless dogs to greener pastures – even though those pastures were an asphalt covered mid-west megalopolis. When Robert called to say his cabin was almost ready, I wasn't as excited as I'd expected I would be. All the miles for work had taken the wind out of my sails for driving, and the more I watched Karma at home, the more I felt bad for wanting to take her away. Still, we were committed to seeing all the lower forty-eight in my mind.

I made some changes. I pulled all the unnecessary stuff off the Rodeo – skid plates, towing package, backseats, anything the machine didn't need to run. I set up a profile on a new social media platform that was focused on picture sharing; it seemed ideal for our trips but, in all that time online, I stumbled into a temptation.

It was Katherine's birthday and I couldn't resist looking her up. I found her but saw no trace of a husband. I hadn't seen or heard from her in years; my heart stopped when I saw her smile. She was working in insurance and living downtown. I scrolled through her photos and all the memories hit me like a light speed tsunami. Almost subconsciously, I sent her a short message:

Happy Birthday!

For days I sat anxiously waiting for a response that never came. Then, it was time to go.

Chapter Nine

We left for New England on a rainy October evening. Karma was pleased with all the extra room she had, but when I stirred the gravel in that old engine, she made straight for her seat. Mom and Dad saw us off, waving us down the road from their driveway. Karma hopped out from her seat near the end of the street and ran to the back glass. She didn't make a sound but sat there watching Mom and Dad get smaller and smaller until we turned off their road and they were gone. She took a big breath and wobbled back to her chair before looking back one more time, then she gave a lick to the hand I had on the shifter, and it was ears tucked back and eyes on the road, ready to see what I had planned for us this time.

We went east to go north. A left turn in Virginia took us through the Shenandoah valley in the night. A full moon was high in the sky and the fog in the valley made silhouettes of all the trees and barns and fences. Those were beautiful miles, all alone on the road, watching flashing white lines pass us by, and moonlit mists swirl in the fields. Karma stayed up late with me on that leg, I wasn't sure if she was taking in the splendor or missing my folks, but she kept looking around in the valley until a few hours before the sun started lighting the sky, then she curled into a ball and started snoring in key with the engine and the hum of our tires on those well-worn roads.

The sun came up through thick clouds over a Mid-Atlantic

Autumn. The wind carried brushstrokes of reds and browns on it's back with swirls of orange and yellow mingled in. It smelled like there was vineyard nearby, the taste of grapes was sweet on the damp morning air. Expectedly, the aromatic bouquet gave way to the noxious fumes of city streets soon enough.

I had decided we'd to drive straight through the core of the Big Apple, but seeing the steel serpent crawling into Manhattan, we opted for a borough. We crossed the Washington Bridge into the Bronx and Karma lit up. Even in New Orleans, I don't think she had ever seen so many people bustling around; I'm not entirely sure I've ever seen that many people. Traffic was awful. Every car length, we had to stop. Poor Karma slammed into the dash, the window frame, her seat back, and finally into the floorboard before she retreated to her bed in the back and gave it up. I had been there a few years after the Towers fell, when there was just a great hole in the Earth where they once stood. It was comforting to see a new spire rising up from the ashes of the twins, but almost impossible to safely appreciate in stop-and-go traffic.

When we finally cleared the city, Karma came back up front. We made a pit-stop in Lowell, Massachusetts; to visit Kerouac's grave. I hadn't picked one up in years, but the spirit of his books was big part of what drove me out onto the road. He'd said it was the mad one's for him, the ones that burned like roman candles in the night. I tidied the littered stone and posed a question to the ghost of it's bearer.

"Was it losing your first love that sent you burning into the night?"

The wind rustled the few leaves that blanketed the dead in that place, but his ghost offered no response. I thought I'd get

Karma's opinion on the matter, but she was fixated on a sign, clearly posted, saying 'no dogs allowed.'

"It's okay sweetheart, you're not a dog, you're a Karma!"

We met Robert north of Boston and he led us to his cabin. It seemed like we were going nowhere, and there was nothing. No houses, no mailboxes, just trees. Then, we pulled up to his cabin on the river and walked down to the water – all up and down the waterway there were little boat docks. He had the place perfectly livable and was just polishing it up to resell. His pup and Karma hadn't forgotten each other, and she welcomed Karma like a sister.

The pups took care of themselves the whole time we were there. He had a doggie door, just barely big enough for Karma's fluffy figure to fit through; but usable. An automatic feeder, a yard with no traffic, and plenty of room to romp in the mostly unfurnished cabin.

We weren't there long before Robert called me out on what he referred to as one of my 'moods'.

"What's her name?"

"How do you do that?!"

"It's a big brother thing, can't you tell when Pete's wheels are turning?"

"That's fair… I guess part of it is thinking about this road family I built and how strown my heart is now - but honestly, it's Kat. She's always been in the back of my mind…"

He gave me a stern, brotherly look before he responded.

"I try to reserve the word for family for people who were there when I was going to the bathroom in my pants and the only way I knew to get food was to cry; and for the people who are gonna be there when it's time for that again."

"Point taken..."

"And last I heard of Kat, she was engaged? That should tell you the woman you loved didn't survive your split. Trust me, I've been through two divorces and I've known you a while on top of that. You're not the same, she's not either, and you don't want any part of that mess."

"Is that how love works, we just start a new character when it faulters?"

"You're in love with a moment from your past, not a real person that exists today. From where I'm sitting, you've got no real obligations, a good base at home, and a good dog at your side. You are as free as a man can be and you should focus on living your life, not looking back at it."

"I think it's a fine line between freedom and loneliness. I mean, are you happy man?"

"I feel like people are born with a range of how happy or sad they can be and they're pretty much stuck with it. I'm as happy as I can be with the brain I drew. I shoot more for fulfillment. Fulfillment can come from lots of places; happiness really just comes from love and that's an ever-dwindling commodity in this world."

"I guess I'm just trying to figure out what comes next."

"Whatever comes next is what comes next. Maybe Kat crosses your path and you get your fairytale sequel. Maybe there's a stranger out here that makes you forget all about Kat. Maybe there's no one. Maybe you don't wake up tomorrow! Life is making it from one maybe to the next and hoping you stumble into something great. There's eight billion people on this rock Mark, it's not really fair to demand one specific person before you'll be satisfied with life."

"Haven't I stumbled enough? I just want what I had..."

"Well suck it up buttercup, cause that ain't how life works."

I was frustrating him, but he could tell he was about to cross from teasing into torment and he softened his tone, in his way.

"If you don't perk up, I'm gonna put you out of your misery and steal Karma. I guarantee you my mutt is thinking the same thing, only she doesn't care whether you perk up or not, she just wants a new sister."

"Well, that's Northern hospitality at its finest."

"Look, nothing's impossible. Maybe the world is just working you two into the perfect pair. God knows you could use some work! Maybe you just need to be patient and wait it out."

"Can we wait at the bar?"

"Now you're talking! Let's head down to Boston and get the Irish out."

In the few days we stayed, Karma and I toured all of New England and caught the final days of autumn's flaming hues sweeping across the region. For all the bright fleeting colors we saw, I found myself mostly admiring the evergreens, the ones that didn't change with the passing of seasons.

I decided, of course, to go the long way home and check off as many states as we could. We drove across New York state toward Buffalo. I couldn't believe how much a place called New York could look like my hometown. Every few miles of hills and trees that passed, there would be someone selling Maple Syrup, arguing that theirs was the best for however many miles around. As we approached Buffalo, we caught a light snow that blanketed the landscape but not the roads, my favorite driving conditions.

I decided to cross into Canada so we could add Michigan to Karma's list of states. Going international with our adventures was just a bonus. After letting Kamra explore her first snow, we pulled out of a Buffalo gas station and into the line at the border crossing. We only had to wait for a car or two, then the border agent saw Karma and asked me to pull over. Karma cast a spell and won the agent's affection, then while they played, another agent searched my stripped-down Rodeo.

"Where's your seats, eh?"

"Pulled them for gas mileage and to give her more room."

"And your skid plates?"

"Just for the weight."

"Smart… but looks suspicious so we have to check."

"Fair enough."

The agent playing with Karma giggled and jumped into the conversation.

"Sweet puppy you got, where you two headed, eh?"

"Taking the long way home from visiting a friend in New England."

I told her about our coast to coast run and how we were trying to get the lower forty-eight done now. Both agents praised Karma's manners and wished us well on our way.

Driving across Canada, I thought I'd found the deal of the century on gas until I realized they sold it in liters, not gallons - then, we crossed paths with a huge flock of birds. They flew in and out of our field of view for miles, all circling each other in the air, making different shapes and patterns in the sky. At one point, I thought I saw Karma in their art.

Under that distraction, I made a wrong turn toward Toronto and we ended up seeing that massive place, and losing two hours. The international episode of our adventures ended far later than intended when we finally arrived at Ambassador Bridge in Detroit.

I pulled up to a toll booth thing and the guy told me to turn my engine off.

"Where have you been?" he barked.

"Heading home from New England."

"What are you carrying?"

"Just Karma."

"Is that your dog?"

"Yes…"

"Where are your seats?"

"Pulled them out to give her more room."

"Why are you this far from home?"

"Just wandering…"

"What was your business in Canada?"

"…taking the scenic route…"

"Please pull forward to the man with the shotgun."

We did as they instructed and they got me out to continue the interrogation. One younger officer was smitten with Karma.

"She sure does love you!" he beamed.

"I sure do love her!"

We went round and round about how I'm just wandering around with my dog, and they pull out this nasty crate and tell me to put Karma in it, and that I can wait inside. I asked if I could wait outside with her on her leash.

"If you wanna stand in the lake winds while we search your car, be our guest…" was the shotgun man's flat reply.

Karma and I went to stand over by the crate and shiver. It wasn't just the cold making me shiver, I was scared.

After about an hour of them dissecting the Rodeo, Karma developing frostbite, and my fingers freezing solid, they waved me over.

"We are bringing the dog, if he doesn't come up with anything, you can go. Meantime, you can put your dog in the crate and step inside if you want."

"I'm fine, thank you."

All their dog smelled was Karma and finally my blue fingers pulled the latch on that Rodeo to let my baby back inside.

I had to go in and fill out some paperwork, where a nice lady explained all the red flags we'd triggered and how one can't just cross international borders with a dog 'willy-nilly'. I thanked her for her service and rushed back to Karma.

I went straight to the Rodeo, started it, and cranked the heat all the way up. Then I heard something hit the back window. Me and Karma both jumped out of our skin and that young agent, the one smitten with Karma, yelled,

"Great dog man, pretty girl! You guys be safe! There's construction on this exit, it's faster if you take the one on the south end of the lot."

I waved our thanks and took his advice. Between that frigid bridge and Ohio, I remember nothing but the burning of my thawing fingers and thinking about facing the reality of using my one phone call to have someone drive up here and bail Karma out of the pound before they euthanized her, all over permits and a line on a map. We didn't stop until we crossed the Michigan line.

We lingered at the first Ohio rest stop for a while. It was a crossroads moment in a filthy bathroom mirror. Did I want to keep wandering from town to town with this pup until we ran out of gas, money, or luck? If not, then what were we doing out here?

When we finally got home, I was a wreck. With fourteen more states under its wheels, the Rodeo wasn't faring too much better. I went back to transporting pups for the shelter. I went back to playing games. I went back to working on the Rodeo, and I went back to having no real goal.

In most games, you will play for a while, finish all your quests beat all your bosses, and then you wait. Every so often, they release new things to do, but in between – at least for me – the game is a bore. I started playing all sorts of indie games, each with its own clever twist and safe little escape. Karma hated every one of them. I reminded her it was better than being stuck at a Michigan border crossing in the cold, and she was content to take that and run to the folks for love and affection.

In between my return and Thanksgiving, Peter negotiated a way out of his lease. We planned to start moving him after Nana's feast and have him settled by Christmas. Nubs had her litter and he picked out a boy that looked just like Big Bill, except without the tail. To my shame, we never made it over there with Karma after the litter was born. Part of it was games, part of it was that I couldn't bear to see her grieve when they were all taken away.

For the first time in years, Nana had every child around her table that Thanksgiving. Ben had made it, and Karma was obsessed with him. I guess I shouldn't have been surprised, he was the first human she ever met, even before me. Still, I almost got jealous at how close she stuck to him. The folks were decidedly jealous.

After gorging myself on turkey and ham, green bean casserole and sweet potatoes, rolls and cranberry sauce and baked mac and cheese, I rose to the challenge of fresh peach cobbler and a few pieces of peanut butter fudge. Miserable, I stepped outside to look at the stars and walk it off. After a while, I heard the door creak.

"You okay out here Sweetpea?"

"Yeah Nana, just ate too much."

She braved the fresh winter air to come stand with me.

"So, where you and your little girl off too next?"

"I don't know Nana. Pete's moving home, we're excited about that. I'm thinkin' we may stick around here for a while and see what happens."

"Well! I like the sounds of that!"

She stepped close and grabbed my hand, I noticed hers was shaking a little

"You cold Nana?"

"Nah baby, my heart is warm as the oven in there."

"I love you, Nana!"

"I love you, Sweetpea! I'm gonna go check on these young'uns, you should come on back in 'for you catch cold."

The next day we started moving Peter home. Behind everything we moved, we found a trove of dust, spiders, and memories. By Christmas, the folks' house was full. Dad, Mom, Me and Karma, Peter, a freshly spayed Nubs, and our new addition, a plump little kitten named Solomon. Karma was in heaven, except for one thing. Solomon. Everyone loved Karma. Everyone except Solomon. I blamed myself for not taking her over there after that litter was born, but I assumed they'd work it out.

She just wanted to love the baby, but she terrified the baby. She would lay over and whine, he would swat and hiss and hide under the couch. Nubs sat on her new perch, the back of the couch, and watched with mild interest, making bets with herself on whether Karma would just gobble the little guy up in frustration.

Karma gave up every night at suppertime. She took her place by my chair and ate the plate we laid down for her. Solly, as we quickly came to call him, did his best to get milk from his mother, but she denied him, as he had denied Karma.

As scared as he was through that whole transition, when it came time to open Christmas presents, he was mortified. The look in Solly's eyes when Karma ripped and shredded those boxes was sheer terror. I wondered if he was imagining himself as the present, being held down under her paws while she used her massive neck and jaws to rip him into tiny little pieces of cat confetti.

After we all opened our gifts, Me and Peter and Karma sat in the floor, playing with our new toys. Mom and Dad were on the couch with Nubs, perched high on its back, while Solly cowered in mortal fear behind it; hissing and clawing at anyone who tried to bring him up for love.

We all found our new place that winter, and Karma was our peacekeeper. She felt when things were getting tense and used her magic along with what she had learned on the road to clear the air as best she could. Sometimes that meant doing something cute, sometimes it was as simple as a lick. Other times, it was making a big mess in the floor to make everyone mad at her instead of each other.

Sitting on the back patio, watching the flowers bloom in the early spring, I started thinking again about where to go and what to do next. I think we always took the holidays to stop worrying about what comes next and focus on appreciating what came before. Daffodils and Dogwood Blossoms were the alarm clocks to that nostalgic slumber. Karma was pacing the yard on her chain, glancing back at me wondering what I was thinking. She trotted up to my side and I just asked her.

"Where should we go next?"

Without hesitation, she walked to the back door and sat

patiently for someone to open it.

"Bloom where you're planted Sweetpea." That was something Nana said when we were kids. I started thinking whatever I was going to do, I was pretty sure I wanted to do it here. Those feelings were soon set in stone by a huge earthquake and tsunami in Japan. It was a time of grief for so many, but I felt saddest for the people living abroad who knew they could never go home again.

Me and Karma were hanging out with Nana weekly during that time. There was an antique mall about a half hour from town that her and Grandpap used to frequent. They allowed dogs so when she mentioned wanting to go, we decided to have an outing. She was telling me stories about her and Grandpap, and about all the dusty things on the shelves. Karma was stirring up dust bunnies and killing bugs that skittered out of the booths. We passed a jewelry booth and I thought about our little bet.

"We never did decide what I owe you if I lose our bet, Nana."

"Our bet?! Oh, your Grandpap's ring?"

"Yes ma'am… so what do you want if I lose?"

"All I ask is that you make a good life for yourself, Sweetpea! Just take good care of your life."

Chapter Ten

Happy Birthday! That was all the message said. It was from Katherine. I was 30 years old and I had no idea what to do.

I pulled Peter aside and showed him the message.

"What should I do man? I don't know what to do!"

Peter looked at me confused.

"I don't know… Maybe say 'thank you'…?"

Peter always knew what to do, so that's what I did. Moments later, I got a response:

Can I buy you a coffee?

I pulled Peter back into huddle,

"What do you think man, what should I do?"

This time he looked at me like I was a blithering idiot.

"It's a simple question brother, give her a simple answer!"

"Right!"

And so, I replied:

Sure, when are you free?

I'm free tonight, how about you?

Yeah! Do you remember that bookshop café?

The one you used to drag me to on every date we ever had? Yesssss, are they even still open?

Yep. Meet you there at 7?

Deal!

When I got to the coffee shop she was nowhere to be found. I got my flavorless latte, sugared it up, and stirred away the frond the barista had made in the froth. I jumped every time the old bell on the door rang. Then, she walked back into my life.

She looked at me and smiled. She was even more beautiful than I remembered, her silky dark hair dancing in the breeze from the door, her deep brown eyes calling me like the sea. All her natural splendor had been refined, and she was nothing short of spellbinding. Stunned, I waved. She held up her finger to ask for a minute and disappeared toward the counter. I couldn't help but notice her ring finger was bare. An eternity and a few moments later, she reappeared with two lattes.

"I know you'll have another; I'll try to keep up." she smiled.

By the middle of her second latte, she was chatting on about work and her friends, and asking a million questions at once about Karma's adventures, all at a thousand words a minute. I was intoxicated by her. The place was 24 hours, so we didn't realize how long we'd sat there until the bar crowd started showing up from having been run off their stools.

"I should probably be letting you get back to Karma."

"I'm sure the folks have her well in hand."

"You're back at your parents?"

"Yeah, regrouping I guess, to be honest I'm not sure what I'm doin' right now."

"…I know how that goes."

"It was nice to see you Kat, I don't want to keep you… I appreciate the coffee and the company."

Her gaze fell away, and almost in a whisper she replied.

"You're welcome."

I took the last sip of my coffee and slid back from the table to leave that flawless moment. She didn't move.

"Mark… Can I ask you something."

"Ask away!"

"Or maybe I need to tell you something… I don't know what I need to do, but you need to be a part of it…"

Her eyes searched the floor and the walls before searching mine, she looked confused.

"Do you ever think about us?"

I felt like it got quieter and everyone in the room was watching, but I didn't care. I knew exactly how I felt but I didn't know what to say, so I just started speaking.

"Kat… not a day has passed I haven't missed you and wished you were with me. I treated you like an actress in the movie of my life or like some game piece on a board and no matter what I try to do with that regret, it remains. I failed you Kat, I failed us. I am so sorry for whatever struggles brought you to this moment and I'm sorry that I am this character in your story, but I love you and-"

"I'm sorry. I have to go!"

Before I could find another word to say, she was already out the door. I ran after her and caught her at her car.

"Kat?!"

"Please go! It's not your fault Mark, but please… just go."

"No! Not until you play fair! You asked me a question and I answered you honestly, now it's my turn… Do you still love me, Kat? Is that why we're here?!"

She turned her dark eyes back toward mine and a mascara-stained tear clung to an eyelash.

"From the moment you walked into my life… I have loved you, Mark… I wanted to see you, I didn't know how it would feel and now that I know, I don't know what to do. Please… go home, I'm so sorry."

I took a step toward her and reached for her hand.

"Don't…"

Our faces fell into mirrored frowns and our gazes turned toward the machines that would carry us home, then we both walked away. No goodbyes, no maybes, just the empty thuds of my footsteps and her car door latching closed. I waited until she started her car and left. Then I went home.

My pride kept me from sadness, Karma kept me from loneliness, and Katherine kept her distance. By Karma's 4th Birthday, I'd convinced myself it had all been a dream.

Peter had taken the job on the old timer's ranch. It wasn't a big factory farm, most of the equipment was family members. The old timer's kids had their fills of farm work growing up, but his grandkids were still worth a few days a week in the fields. When I wasn't running transports, I was helping out there. We would come home reeking of manure and had to set up a changing station in the garage. To me it was a smelly bridge to the next maybe. To Peter, it was a path to a new life.

Way back in the wooded part of the ranch, there was this old shack. It was part of the original farmstead the owner's so-many-greats grandfather had built after the family first bought the place. The old man had nearly forgotten about it until they harvested the timber and was figuring he should probably tear it down to free up the land. Still, he hated the thought of demolishing the building where it all began for his family.

The old guy remembered playing around in the shell of the house when he was a kid and took up several of Peter's afternoons telling stories from the old days. Peter convinced him to keep it – he told the old man he would fix it up on the condition that he would let Peter live in it after.

When I finally met him, this guy was the most cantankerous, curmudgeonly, crotchety old man I ever saw. Zero patience, zero manners, zero happiness. That was at first. Then, I saw something else. Something in the old timer's eyes when his ancient mutt made a clockwork trot to his side and they both lit up at his wife's frail voice rustling like dry leaves through the hall.

"Who's here? Is it Thelma?!"

The old man's response sounded like it came from another person, a younger man, a gentle, serene, happy man.

"Just this Pete kid come to look at the old shack, Love."

"Bring him in! Bring him in! There's a week's wortha food cooked!"

His wife, his dog, that farm - they were his world. The only thing this guy really wanted to do in life was to be with that woman and that dog on their farm. We were interrupting his good times, and he was just protecting what was left of them by being short with us.

I couldn't see the same silver linings in Peter's ruins. It looked unholy with all those felled trees laying around drying and their stumps strewn like tombstones across the field. It was framed like a warehouse palette and the roof and walls were shot. Literally, shot with guns.

"Are you sure you don't wanna just put this thing out of its misery man?"

"It's just broken. Broken things need love too. All it takes is time."

"I'm pretty sure this rotting carcass is the result of time."

"Time is the currency of love and life, brother. I'm gonna rip everything out then buildout inside the old shell and have utilities put in. Help me get this sheet metal on the roof… I'm thinkin' I'll do a wraparound porch and when I buy this whole farm, you and Karma can always stay here on your travel breaks."

We dragged the razor-sharp sheet of corrugated steel off his truck and up on the roof. There was no door, the windows were filled with jagged teeth of broken glass, there were bullet holes in the walls and all manner of strange bugs crawling around - but he had a roof over his head.

There was a lot going on in the folks' house, but it was a different going on than at Peter's old house. Grown-up goings on. The folks were always rushing here or there to see this or buy that, Peter stayed later and later working on that shack until it was livable for him. Then, his room started emptying. It was odd, not like a sudden move where you pack everything up and you say goodbye – it was a slow erosion of presence, like a stream pulling silt away from a bank until the course of the water was changed.

Whatever spare time I had, I spent with Karma or exploring the virtual worlds of my games. By the time we got to Nana's table, the only thing I was curious about outside my dragon-filled realms was whether Ben had been part of the team that got Bin Laden or not.

"Can't take credit on that one Cuz."

"If you had done it, could you tell me?"

"Nope. But since I didn't, I can - wasn't me."

One of my favorite things to do in a game was hoard and sell loot. One of my favorite things to do at Nana's was look at the hoard of loot her and Grandpap had gathered in all their years of antiquing. She caught me sifting through it that night.

"Whatcha doin' Sweetpea?"

"Just looking at your collection out here."

"It's just all the stuff that don't mean nuthin' to me, I need to have your daddy sell it all off in the yard."

"You don't want any of this stuff?!"

"Everything that means somethin' to me is in the house."

My first thought was that I could wander the country selling it all off for her, but gas prices burst that bubble right quick. Then, on a whim, I asked.

"What if I opened a little shop Nana, would you let me sell some of it for you?"

"Sweetpea, you can throw a match an' gas too it for all I care! I been through it all an', for the life of me, I can't remember where or how we got most of it."

Antiques had been a part of our family since I was born, both sets of grandparents were collectors, and everyone had their own little hoards of dusty junk stashed away in their garages. I figured it couldn't be much different than running a video store and that all I needed was a place to sell out of. Once again, I left my Nana's Thanksgiving with a dream and goal.

There was a vacant building in town. It looked like an Asian castle, with a large open space on the ground floor and an apartment on the smaller second floor. The owner knew Dad and had been struggling to get a renter. The previous tenant was a donut shop and the remnant sugar and flour made it almost impossible to keep bugs out. Within a month, I had an affordable retail space and a free apartment, products to sell, and a license to sell them.

By Valentines Day, Karma and I had moved and were both struggling to adjust to living by ourselves. I was putting pieces of other people's pasts on the shelf while trying to keep my mind off my own. That's when I realized what it meant to be 30.

I bent over to pick up a six-ounce doll with dark hair. For a split second, I thought of Katherine. Then, my mind rushed toward all the things that needed doing to get the shop ready. As I went to stand up, I fell to the floor. It felt like someone had skewered my leg with a flaming spear. I started sweating, it was hard to breathe, I felt drunk from the pain. I rolled myself over and tried to get up, but I couldn't straighten out or put any weight on my leg. When the pain finally waned, I crawled over to a two-wheel dolly and climbed to my feet on it. Hunched over that dolly, I wheeled myself to the phone and called the folks. They drove me to the Doctor.

"Welcome to your mid-life!"

That's what the doctor said. I'd pulled a muscle in my back, and it was pinching a nerve. It was weeks of barely being able to get out of bed and terrifying Karma with my yelps any time she bumped into me. My chief partner in crime on the shop was Dad and he and Karma picked up all the slack while I was recovering.

When I finally got back on my feet, Pops was with me every day, telling me what he knew about whatever we pulled from the crispy cardboard boxes. Second in command was Karma. Thoroughly shredding those crispy boxes so that we could fit them all neatly in the dumpster.

"Hey, here's a set of Encyclopedia Brittanica! I heard they are printing it for the last time this year."

"Yeah, I saw that on the news."

"This set was made the year your mother and I got married."

"I hope they had a better run of it than you and Mom did."

I had said it without even thinking, but I'd opened a door.

"I'm sorry you boys had to watch us struggle all those years."

"I didn't mean anything by that Pop, I'm just a little overwhelmed by this project. It spilled over."

"No... You're right. Our marriage wasn't always pretty to watch."

"Are any of them?"

He sat down by a stack of dinner plates that had fed decades of families. He looked sad and I thought he might be thinking about the friends he lost recently, members of his breakfast club, men he'd known for decades. That wasn't it.

"Pa and Grannie argued... but they went to the barn. When they came back inside, they would sit at the table and sip coffee and talk until they were laughing with each other again. They came through the Depression and, I think, they weren't afraid to really need each other. Your mother and I came up through different times. Our generation decided love needed to make sense and people needed to be independent."

He picked up another dish from a box and flipped it over to look at the maker's mark.

"That's not so bad Pop, I think my generation just gave up on love."

We sat there surrounded by silent forgotten things that had seen this drama play out over and over as they'd moved through the homes of strangers on their way to that floor. Dad stopped being my father for a moment and we were just two men, pondering life.

On opening day, I got up and poured Karma a bowl of meat cereal, made myself the only hot meal I knew how to make at the time – eggs – and filled my Grandpap's thermos. We climbed down the metal staircase to our new shop and stood for a moment in front of the door. It didn't feel the way I had expected. I put the key in the lock, opened the door, flipped the OPEN sign on, and turned on the lights. Then we walked behind the counter and Karma curled up in the bed I'd put there for her and got herself back to sleep while I worked on deciding if I'd made the right decision.

I was doing my best to be upbeat, but on day one of my new adventure, I felt overwhelming doubt. I decided to walk the floor and got five steps out of sight from the door when the old bell I'd installed over it jingled. I heard Karma go wild trying to get enough traction on the concrete floor to get to our first customer.

"Don't mind the pup, she just want's your attention or your food!"

I could hear Karma's claw clattering on the floor in excitement, they muffled the customer's voice.

"So I see!"

It didn't sound like anyone I knew. Then she giggled.

"Do you have Karma T-shirts?"

I took five steps back toward the door before I replied, to be sure my mind wasn't playing tricks on me. She was right there, rubbing on Karma's ears, and Karma was approving.

"No… we don't have those yet… I'm sorry"

"Oh, well it'd be a good thing to get."

"…I'll have to try and get that done."

"Mary told me an old friend was opening a new antique store… I guess I thought I might see if he needed any help."

"I… Well… Karma, this is Kat… Kat, this is Karma."

"Pleased to meet you, Karma!"

Karma was already in love with her.

"It's really good to see you, Kat."

She stepped forward, arms open for a hug that bloomed into a kiss. I was lost in her warmth, then she brought me back with a whisper.

"It's good to see you too, mister. Now, why don't you show me around this store of yours?"

Kat was living in her brother's guestroom and found her way up our stairs more nights than not. The folks were demanding that I bring our new roommate to Karma's 5th Birthday party, but Kat wasn't too keen to go.

"I'll be here when you guys get back and we can have an after-party!"

"Did you hear that Karma, you get an after-party this year!"

She raised her head and turned her eyes up to Kat for advice on what to do.

"I'll be right here sweetheart; you go open your presents with your grandparents!"

Karma's head fell back onto Kat's lap and out of the corner of her eye she gave me a look that pleaded for me to just say 'stay'.

When I finally did get her to follow me to the door, she made Kat feel awful by standing there looking at her like 'are you coming?!'

"I'm sorry sweetheart, I promise, next year! You go with Daddy." Kat replied.

I was happy it was Karma's birthday, but mostly the smile on my face at that party was Kat's promise of a next year.

By the end of summer, Peter called me up to report that he

had driven the last nail into his cottage and invited me and Karma out to visit. I'd only been out once since I'd helped him patch the roof. It was incredible what he'd done.

The decaying ruin he'd started with was now a remodel-show worthy cottage. He filled it with old things he'd gotten from my shop, things he'd reclaimed from the trash piles on the farm, and things he had built. He had a spot set aside for next year's garden and the old farmer's chickens had taken to hanging out in his little area of the farm. Karma was unsure what to do with nothing between her and the chickens. Within a few minutes, she remembered; the only reasonable thing to do was chase them.

When she exhausted herself of chasing the chickens, she found a tree limb as tall as me and came dragging it to Peter's wraparound porch with her head held high and eyes full of pride at the monster stick she'd found. Then, she set to work trying to make mulch of it while Peter and I rocked away the final hours of the country afternoon in his handmade chairs. The calm of that place seemed unbreakable, and I found myself almost jealous when we left.

Chapter Eleven

My place was in the middle of town, between the main highway and the railroad tracks. Peace had to be imported. There was always the sound of traffic or train horns, sirens, someone's loud music, the bells of the church on the other side of the tracks. Even in all that ruckus, peace could be found. Sometime in the smallest hours of the morning while the whole town slept, or in a quiet visit from Kat under the halo of TV light, even in the white noise of Karma snoring. Peace could be found.

Business picked up in the fall and the shop was a close second for the most popular topic at Thanksgiving. There was trouble in the world, so Ben was the clear winner for most popular person to corner and question.

"Are we going into Crimea?"

"What's going on in the Middle East?!"

"What do you think about Cuba?"

He did his best to answer and Nana just sat and smiled, giving Karma bits of her uneaten turkey while we all stuffed ourselves with desserts. Later, Ben decided to join me and Karma outside to escape the family security briefing.

"How you been Cuz?"

"I'm good man, it's good to have ya home!"

"Good to be here!"

"I was listening to you talk in there. I haven't had much

time for news with all the old stuff I've got to sort through. Sounds like a mess out there."

"Is what it is Cuz… job security, I guess. Speaking of news, where's Kat?"

"Ha! I see the family rumor mill opened a west coast branch."

"Intelligence is part of my job description, Cuz. You know how we do."

"She's eating with her family, first year back together and all…"

"Nana told me she hasn't seen her yet. She remembers her from the old days though."

"I'll take the blame for that. I'm selfish with our time and I'm not sure I trust our wild tribe to not scare her away!"

"What's Karma think of her?"

"Karma would leave me in a heartbeat for Kat – it kinda hurts my feelings."

At the mention of her name, Karma abandoned her patrol of the yard and came over to Ben for love and/or leftovers.

"You heard her mama died?"

"Oh man, I hadn't! I loved her! I'm sorry to hear that…"

"Yeah, not sure what happened, thinkin' she got into poison at that farm out behind my dad's place."

"I am sorry man…"

"It's just part of life. So, when are y'all gettin' back on the road?"

"I don't know man. Pete and I talked about a quick trip to see Tom at his new place. I still think about finishing the lower forty-eight, but I feel anchored here with the shop and Kat."

"Anchors aren't bad things to have."

"I'd trust a sailor to know. I guess we'll just see where the winds and the tides take us… I'm gonna get back in here for seconds on desert, you comin'?"

"I'll be in in a minute."

I opened the door with a long creak and Karma trotted inside. Ben's gaze never left the yard.

"Hey, Cuz… do you remember playing football out here with Grandpap?"

"Of course! Those were good times man!"

"…The best."

Starting on Black Friday there was a constant flow of people in and out of my shop. Unfortunately, there was no matching flow of money in and product out. Everyone wanted to come to remember.

"My mother had a whole set of these." One would say.

"My dad used to collect those." Chirped another.

"I remember the first time I saw that!"

"I'd totally forgotten about this!"

On and on they went, then on to the next shop with their wallets full. The only occasional break from that broken record was:

"What a great dog!"

As much as Nana looked forward to Thanksgiving, and Mom looked forward to Christmas, I was looking forward to New year. No party, no music. Just Karma, Kat, and cable TV.

We stayed extremely busy doing nothing. We just sat, wrapped in blankets on the couch with Karma sandwiched between us, enjoying each other's warmth and company. We decided to try a streaming service instead of cable for our TV and binge watched the year away. Kat's resolution was to finish her business degree. Karma and I said we were going to improve the shop and get rid of the bugs. We both looked forward to the year ahead with a sense of hope that this was the beginning of our new lives, together. When the ball dropped, they both looked my way with their big brown eyes. To Karma's disgust, Kat got the first kiss of that year.

I converted my shop into a mall and picked up some work at a restaurant down the street to make ends meet. I was meeting lots of new people by renting space out to locals and I was learning to cook – which Kat adored. She started school and poor Karma got neglected, but she never complained. When Peter decided he wanted to make that trip to see Tom in Texas, I was ready for a vacation from the shop and Karma was ready for some undivided attention. I secretly wanted Kat to go, but I knew she was going to be busy with school stuff and didn't ask. Before we set dates, I called Tom to check in.

"What about Karma, bro?" was his third question.

"I was thinkin' of leaving her with the folks."

"She's welcome to come with you guys, my roommate has a 2-year-old Great Dane that could use a playmate."

"Does your boy not play with him?!"

"I had to put Karma's pops down bro, he was eat up with cancer."

"Man… I'm sorry to hear that."

"I miss him, I'm not even gonna try to lie. He was my buddy, but life moves forward with or without us, y'know."

"…So, everyone will be cool if I bring Karma?"

"Honestly bro, I'll be disappointed if ya don't."

In two weeks, we were back on the road again with a new member of the crew. Peter had Karma's seat and she was miserable over it. After about 100 miles she finally accepted her lot and found a comfortable place sitting on the backseat floorboard with her paws up on the console, turning to Peter when he spoke and to me when I spoke, like a kid sitting there listening to all the conversations the grown-ups were having.

We got to Tom's in the night. Karma and the Great Dane made fast friends and Peter and I did the same with all Tom's roommates. There were four of them in total. Each played a different instrument, and they had a studio set up in the living room. It was like a Texas version of Peter's old place. Bigger. But everything's bigger in Texas.

Our second night there, the guys had a jam session and invited a bunch of their friends over. I noticed Karma hanging close to a cute girl across the room. Peter noticed her, too. It looked like he was telling her all Karma's stories and she was hanging on every word. Karma eventually made her way back to me and I noticed Peter and Karma's cute friend had vanished.

We made a trip to see Samuel and his family on our last day. The little boys were well on their way to being little men, and the bump in his wife's belly was now a little girl in her arms. Karma remembered the boys and galloped to them. She sniffed and licked them from head to toe. They loved her, but she'd lost her hold on their hearts, they now belonged to their little sister.

When it was time to get back home, I was ready. Peter, on the other hand, was not. I noticed he kept fiddling with his phone those first miles out of the Lone Star State, then he just took to staring out the window with a smile on his face.

"How are you and Kat?" he asked without looking.

"This whole time we've been down here… all I've been thinkin' about is gettin' back to her. If that tells you anything."

"We figured that's what was on your mind."

"How are you and that cutie?"

"Rose…" he said as he looked my way.

"Rose, is it? Is she what's got the farm boy fiddling with his fancy tech all the way home so far?"

"Yep. I'll be honest with you brother; we've both been thinkin' about what's waiting for us at home. I love my place and the life I've got going there, but…"

"But?"

"But I'm going back to an empty house."

He turned again to watch the blur of the arid landscape slowly yielding to greener pastures.

"I miss the life in our old place, the people, the animals, the smell of stale smoke, litter boxes, and kerosene. Just the life in it. Part of the reason I wanted to take this trip was to get away from the emptiness of my house."

"Have you thought about gettin' a pup? I can only highly recommend it!"

"No doubt, Karma was the best decision you ever stumbled through. But honestly, I think I wanna start a little higher on the food chain. Every mile you put between me and Texas, there's this feeling… I don't know, it's stupid."

"Man… Pops and I had a conversation not too long ago, a real conversation. I think we concluded that none of it makes any sense, and it's not supposed to."

"It's hard imagining Dad saying anything like that, I have to hear about this."

I told him all about the conversation I'd had with Dad on the floor of my shop, he cataloged every word and when the story reached its end, he'd reached his conclusion.

"I'm just gonna keep up with her and see where it goes, I don't know why I'm even stressing it."

"People want love to be logical and It's not, it's magical or spiritual or something. Completely out of our hands. That's where I'm at with it."

He laughed from the pit of his belly.

"Who are you and what have you done with my brother?!"

"Down inside me, there's a frightened five-year-old that wakes up every day wanting to run, terrified all these things he loves are going to be taken from him and wanting to deny the world that theft... I'm still your brother, I think I might just be growing up slightly."

It had been a long time since the Rodeo had to put that many miles down at once. When she started heating up, I hoped it was just a last-minute temper tantrum. 119 miles from our door, I finally pushed her too far. The engine started steaming and hissing and smoking and we had no choice but to pull over. A quick check of the map revealed a state park two miles ahead. After a break on the shoulder, we got back on the road, but the stalwart Rodeo was instantly burning up again. As we coasted off the freeway into the park, the engine started making all sorts of squishy clattering noises, then... it quit.

It was late, but Peter knew a guy that worked for a towing service. He called and the guy agreed to come get us with no emergency fee if we didn't mind waiting a bit. We sat in the park for several hours, Karma wandered around while Peter picked on his guitar. I looked at the caged birds they had there, but mostly I just worried.

We finally got home in the middle of the night and the folks came out to welcome us. We pushed my busted wagon back into the garage and Peter carried us back to our empty apartment, then he went back to his empty house. I knew Kat would be over tomorrow and I had Karma there to ease my worries about the Rodeo, but I felt a little sorry for my little brother. I had been so proud of everything he had done at the cottage that I never really thought about what he had sacrificed for it.

I was short on money and couldn't go more than a week without wheels. Kat and I spent that next day looking for something cheap when we came across a minivan for seven hundred dollars. The ad said:

'Sound mechanical condition, interior extensively damaged from raising five kids.'

When we got there to see it, I suddenly realized Karma was, in fact, not one of the most destructive forces on the planet. When I saw how much easier she could get in and out, and all the extra space I would have to move boxes, I had to have it. I felt like the only way to resolve my problem was to sell or scrap the Rodeo, but Kat wouldn't have it. She insisted on paying for the van in case we needed to haul kids around one day.

Karma's 6th birthday rolled around, and it was the same old setup. Same old Karma ripping open presents and trying to get food off the table, same old family laughing around the table, but there were new things. There was a silver Minivan in the driveway, waiting to carry Karma and all her presents home, and there was an extra chair around the table that year, right next to mine. It held a dark-haired belle, nervously sitting with Karma at her feet while my family was falling in love with her.

Kat was raised a city girl; I grew up a farm-town boy. When she asked to take a trip the night of Karma's party, I was surprised she just wanted to go back home.

Karma grew up a travelling dog and while she listened to this conversation, you could see the excitement building in her eyes. Kat had learned Karma's language well.

"I'm sorry Karma, Mommy and Daddy are taking a little trip without you."

We just stayed in Kat's old neighborhood for a weekend. Over three days we visited places she remembered, several places she'd lived, the schools she used to attend, restaurants she used to love. We had dinner at an old-school drive-up burger joint where she used to eat when she was a kid. I could see the little girl in her come out when she got her burger and shake with a side of tater-tots.

"I used to sit here and think about what I wanted to be when I grew up." She confessed.

"What did you wanna be?"

"It was different every day."

"Sounds like me! What do you wanna be when you grow up today?"

"Promise you won't laugh?"

"Swear!"

"After my time in insurance and my trip through the legal system, I think I wanna be an attorney and work the other side of the line. People need help- …why are you laughing!?!"

"Only because, of all the things I could do with my life, nothin' would make my father happier than me being married to a lawyer!!"

She slapped my arm and made the most adorable pouting face you ever saw, Karma had taught her well.

"So, what about you, mister? What're you gonna be when you grow up?"

"I wish I knew baby… I could live in a cardboard box, and

if you and Karma were there, I'd call it winning!"

"Babe! We couldn't live in a cardboard box… Karma would eat it."

She had met me in my hometown. She had seen the world and the people that made me, and while her past wasn't a mystery to me, I had never seen it. That trip was the best, days and nights of holding hands, cuddling, laughing about old times and enjoying all the memories we had shared in our lives. I felt so close to her there, like we were two people living one life.

On our way home we talked about how the city had changed in just a few years. I mentioned all the places and things that were gone from when we were younger, she talked about all the new skyscrapers going up and all the new restaurants we had. When we arrived and Karma ran for Kat first, it felt like the perfect homecoming.

Jude called with news after we got back. There was a long silence after I asked how he was. In a voice riddled with terror he replied

"She's havin' a litter…"

"Your dogs are boys?!"

"MARY!!!"

"Oh… WHAT!?"

"Yeah! Twins!"

"Uhh… Congratulations… I think."

"Yeah, thanks dude. So, we talked to Tom and got him ordained as a minister online and he's comin' up here to get us hitched – can you make it out to be best man?"

Tom had taken my place as Jude's person to spend hours debating faith and life with, trying to make sense of our world. It hurt me to tell Jude that as much as I would love to, and as honored as I was, I just couldn't get away again so soon. I hated that I couldn't go, and I was a little jealous of their families beginning. The pictures they sent after only made it worse.

Chapter Twelve

The old church out behind the store always played bells over its loudspeakers on the hour. Around Halloween, they switched to playing a few bars of different carols each hour. I was taking the trash out and 'Oh, Little Town' rang out into the night. Normally the sound of the bells told me the time, the sound of those took me back in time. Back to being a kid at Nana's house with Grandpap and all the aunts, uncles, and cousins. Kids running around the house and parents sitting around the table. Nana would keep an eye out for treats boiling over in the kitchen, Grandpap kept an eye out for tempers boiling over in the TV room. I dropped the lid on the dumpster, and it snapped me back to the present. It was freezing outside but I just barely noticed, the cold isn't so bad when your heart is warm.

I looked up at the light glowing though my apartment window, down at all the shelves of memories holding it up. It was a wonderful feeling having everything I loved in one place, I felt like that old farmer of Peter's would be proud. At the same time, it was a little scary.

I thought about the girls up there trying to stay in the one warm spot near the space heater, about the roaches that mainly stayed upstairs, but away from Karma, in the winter. Karma was an expert roach hunter. Even though we discouraged her, she could entertain herself endlessly chasing those nasty things around the apartment and squashing them in her mouth before coming over to collect her payment in kisses. I had always let her lick me in the face and that was the first time it bothered me. Kat didn't allow face licking and called me out on it.

"Babe! She's been licking her butt her whole life before she kisses you, is a roach any more or less disgusting?"

She was right of course. But she never complained about any of it, she just kept bringing her light into our lives.

I made my way up the rusty metal stairs to the apartment, imagining one of the girls falling, or the whole creaking thing just collapsing underneath them. The heartwarming smell of dust cooking off a heater that's been stored away for three seasons greeted me at the door and all my worry turned back to wonderment at what had.

Kat had curled herself up on one end of the couch with a blanket and her laptop. Karma was somewhere under the blanket curled up with her, making it hard to tell what was Kat and what was dog. Kat had her hair up in a ball, right on top of her head, and her glasses on, right at the bottom of her nose. She had on an old T-shirt she'd grabbed from my cleanish laundry and a pair of black yoga pants that Karma had covered in fur. It was extra insulation Kat said. The glasses set the look off, she hated wearing them, but they perfectly complimented the focused look on her face and the pen she blamed Karma for chewing whenever she caught herself gnawing it during a frantic study session.

Karma ran interference for her any time she stayed. If Kat was studying, Karma would rush to the door and act extra excited to see me. She'd run up and sit, shake her head and lick my hand, bump into me a time or two and give me a good sniff. She would walk right next to my feet and if I tried to get more than a little peck off Kat's cheek while she was studying, Karma would demand my attention. On the other hand, if Kat was cooking or watching TV, Karma might acknowledge my arrival with a quick tail wag, or less.

I told Kat that Nana had heard we were together again and was eager to see her. I asked if she would come to Thanksgiving with me and she got visibly nervous about it.

"Can I just stay here with Karma while you go eat?"

"Karma is coming!"

Her face betrayed a certain guilt that my dog was going, and my girlfriend was not, so I decided to press her on it. I told her that we were starting a new tradition, we would be exchanging presents on Thanksgiving to free up time for everyone at Christmas, so there'd be distractions with the kids and Karma opening those and we could just watch from the corner. She coyly conceded that since I hadn't bought that years record-breaking crime game, she would return the favor and go with us.

The afternoon leading into the meal was like that twelve days song. We baked her dessert twice, she redid her makeup three times, changed her outfit four times, asked if we had everything five times. We had sent Karma ahead with Peter for sake of the food and when I called to let them know we were running late, Peter told me that he had to banish Karma from the tree after she mistook one of the great-grandkids presents for her own.

The first chance Nana got to sit down and start talking to Kat was the last chance I got to talk to either of them all night. They jumped right in the middle of Karma and the kids and kept them entertained while the rest of us ate in peace for the first time since my cousins started having babies.

When we gathered to open presents, Kat and Nana got their plates and sat down to watch from the table. The kids ripped their presents apart and Karma made sure their paper was torn down to trash friendly scraps. I caught bits and pieces of Kat and Nana chatting. Nana told Kat about the early holidays she remembered, after the Depression, when the meal was the present. Kat shared her own memories of early holidays, not too far removed from Nana's. They carried on that whole night talking about their lives, their families, and - of course - me.

Karma followed us around while we picked up all the trash, making sure she had torn it all down the smallest shreds she could make. With all the evening's scraps collected and at the road, Peter looked my way with a grin on the way back.

"I think Nana likes your girl."

"I think my girl likes Nana; she hasn't spoken to me all night!"

"That's not a bad thing."

"I try not to think about it too much, but I can't even believe my life right now. It's kind of scary, like, how did I get this lucky?"

"Well don't start thinkin' about it now Brother! She's in there and you should be too."

We sat and watched the kids being kids, the parents being parents, and Karma being Karma. She exhausted herself to the point we basically had to carry her out, so the folks invited her to their place for the night to spare her having to climb the stairs. To be polite, they said she could bring two guests. I was telling Karma it was okay to go with them, and Kat squeezed my arm a little. Her faint smile and brightened eyes said she'd like a little more family time.

We stayed that night in what had been my room with Karma

as our chaperone. It was about the same as I had left it, except they had pushed the bed against the wall to make room for a pile of nick-nacks Dad had stowed in there. Kat fell right to sleep and lay there all night motionless with a little smile on her face. The TV filled the room with the silver light of George Bailey's life and I watched every lovely thing rest until the sun rose through the window.

We had the folks watch Karma for us on New Year's Eve so we could check out a party downtown, but we were back to pick her up before midnight and ended up watching the countdown with them then just spent the night there again. When we got up for the day, we were alone. Me, Kat, Karma, and somewhere out there, Nubs and Solly were hiding from this stranger in my bed.

Kat woke up unsure of where she was for a second. Karma was in her spot between us but the look on her face and the subtle whine in her breath said she was ready to go out. I took her outside and Kat went to wash her face. We met in the kitchen, and Kat picked up a note that said,

'Happy New Year! Help yourselves to the fridge and stove, it was so nice to have you again!'

Kat opened the fridge and cried out,

"SCORE!"

When I turned to look, she was combing the shelves and drawers, rustling bags and reading jars, her smile growing with every new discovery. She paused for a moment and looked at me blankly.

"I'll call you when it's done."

"Huh?"

"To the couch, mister! Karma, take him away."

Karma looked at Kat, looked at me, and after a quick peek

in the fridge, walked toward the couch. She sat down beside it, looked at the cushion, looked at me, then looked back at the cushion again.

We hadn't said it since the night at the café, I don't think I ever stopped thinking it, but we hadn't said it and I wasn't sure why. It felt like it was time.

"Katherine-"

"Couch mister! Your mom stocks a fierce pantry."

"…I love you."

Her motion slowed to a halt. She took a step back and sat down the assortment of things she had gathered on the table, then she walked up to me and placed one hand on each side of my face before floating up onto her toes. With her eyes closed and a beaming smile, she kissed me.

"I have always loved you Mark Andrew… and I will always love you."

She tilted her face down and floated back to the ground, resting her hand on my shoulders and her head on my chest. After a shared breath, she turned up to look at me with narrow eyes and a grin, then with a finger poked into my chest she ordered,

"Now you go watch TV while I make us breakfast."

"Yes Ma'am."

We sat and ate - our chairs pulled impractically close together so that I alternated between eating left-handed and letting Kat feed me when I dropped food. Karma sat quietly under the table waiting for the food I was dropping.

Kat explored the old family photos lining the walls and dug through my old room. She found my old CD collection and stacked up some of her favorites from our youth. We dragged the DVD player close enough to swap out discs, then she laid next to me on the couch, and we let the music take us back to being teenagers again. Karma stole Solly's overstuffed, but still undersized bed, and we listened and slept away our New Year's Day.

Back at home, Karma was starting to check herself more on the steps up to the apartment. They were the metal kind with holes. We took our time up and down them as the new year began. My situation was dependent on the shop, keeping it profitable made living in the apartment above it possible and while the holidays had been good, overall sales were falling. One of the law firms Kat had spoken to hired her as an assistant; she dealt with the worst parts of people's worst days. Divorces, custody, all that sort of thing. Karma could tell when something Kat had to process bothered her personally and did her best to be of comfort.

Even with her nose buried in her laptop and books Kat would be on the couch petting Karma while she read. I complimented her on it once and she said it soothed her too.

"She helps me remember… Just be here, now."

I'd mentioned her moving in before her classes started back up, but she wanted a place closer to school and work. I was a little disappointed, but relieved in a way to not be responsible for us getting evicted if the shop fell apart, or her getting hurt if the building fell apart.

Then the Snowbirds came. Flocks of people that go south to vacation homes in the winter and migrate back north in the spring, stopping at every antique shop they find on the way. By the time they finished their migration, I'd had to leave my restaurant job, my bank accounts were full, my name was out there, and Peter wanted to travel. It was funny, I'd always been so eager to go anywhere, anytime, especially with my brother. And yet, when I agreed to go with him, it may be the first time

I felt obligated to travel.

It was a ranch out in Wyoming where they taught ways to make more of your land. Peter had fully committed to a rancher's life and was becoming more essential to the daily activities of the old timer's farm. He and Rose had quietly kept in touch and even more quietly made trips to see each other. He said he wanted to get some education under his belt and some time with his brother before things, hopefully, got more serious with Rose and work.

It was an out and back trip, just a few nights on the road to get him there and settled, a few nights to hang out. Then I would drive back, and he would fly home when he finished his classes. Kat volunteered to help watch Karma, Dad volunteered to work at the shop. When I left the apartment, it hurt to stand there with my bags packed and look at them just sitting on the couch. What hurt even more was that Karma was completely unconcerned with my departure.

Somewhere in the flats of west Kansas, Peter dropped a perfectly meaningless conversation about the video games we used to play and asked if I wanted to see Yellowstone.

"Absolutely I want to see Yellowstone!"

"We can drop my stuff at the ranch, get some sleep and head over there. It's just a few hours."

The ranch was something like 10,000 acres of rolling hills and scrubby brush. The company had converted an old motel into a bunkhouse. What I saw next makes it hard to remember much else about that trip.

Yellowstone was like a game world made real, nowhere Karma and I had gone, nowhere I had even seen in pictures compared to the otherworldly look of that place. Peter and I barely spoke, we were in awe of what we were seeing around every bend in the road. Steaming landscapes, gurgling geysers, roaming buffalo, wolves, and bears. Everywhere the smell of sulfur and pine. At one point on Mammoth Terrace, Peter just looked over at me wide-eyed and stammered.

"Man, I feel like we're on the moon."

He was right, it was all so strange looking, like we'd been teleported to another planet. I wondered what the first moon landers said about the view, if its alien beauty was diminished by being impossible to share with all the people they loved. The beauty of Yellowstone was beyond description and I was glad to share it with Peter, but surveying all that natural splendor made it crystal clear to me, that the most beautiful things I would ever see were all waiting at home for me.

I decided to leave early and detour for a stayover with Jude and Mary. It was good to see them, but the two new arrivals came after two departures. They had to put both their pups to rest before the kids got there. It was a hard choice for them, One had failed from old age and the other had a stroke shortly after. With two newborns on the way, they felt like it was fate making room in their lives.

"We're moving back home as soon as our lease is up dude."

"That's awesome man, it'll be like old times with the four of us hangin' out together again!"

He panned across the room to his baby boy and his baby girl.

"The six of us… and no, it won't!"

We did our best to hold our laughs and not wake his little bundles of stress and joy. There wasn't much rest to be found there and after a night, I was back on the road to the most amazing attraction in the country… Home.

Suddenly, my little girl was turning 7. We were meeting everyone at the folks', where Karma had been staying all week while I was down at Kat's new place helping her move in. It was Kat's second dog birthday and although the first was puzzling and awkward for her, she jumped right into the celebration this time. Kat and Dad talked law, Mom was engaged with Karma, and I just sat and watched my family enjoying a day. When Karma decided she needed Kat's attention, Mom came over to me.

"Katherine looks so pretty! Thank you for bringing her."

"She insisted really."

"Karma loves her, are you jealous."

"Sometimes… Hey, how is Nana? Pops mentioned she had to go to the doctor."

"…We got some bad news about Nana; the doctors think she's got Parkinson's."

"Is that what's causing that shake in her hand? I thought that was something you got from getting hit in the head too many times."

"That's Parkinson's Syndrome, they think Nana has Parkinson's Disease. It's early and they say everyone progresses through it differently, but we're all worried-"

Kat pulled up a seat beside me.

"Thanks for bringing me!"

She dropped a tender kiss on my cheek. Karma made her way over to inspect the area for leftovers.

"And thank you for having me!" Kat said in a sing-song voice.

Kat leaned toward Karma and let Karma lick her right in the mouth. I could not resist reminding her what she used to say to me when I did that.

"Eww! You kiss your boyfriend with that mouth?"

She brought her lips all the way to my face, then stuck her tongue out and gave me a cartoonish lick on my lips, immediately fleeing to the kitchen before I had a chance to retaliate. Karma chased after her and the two ended up playing hide-and-seek while we cleaned up Karma's mess.

I thanked the folks and announced that it was time to go. Karma paid me no heed and when her Grammie asked if she wanted to spend the night again, there were no objections from either side.

When we got in the van, Kat reached across the console for my hand.

"Is everything okay? Your mom looked worried about something, and I heard you say Nana…"

"They think that shaking is Parkinson's. Mom said it's early, they don't know a lot right now."

Seeds of tears sparkled into her eyes and she clutched my hand and whispered "No". She didn't let go until we were home.

Chapter Thirteen

Jude and Mary moved back home. Even with their kids, it was like old times, four people who knew each other when they were all just learning to be themselves. Instead of gossiping and flipping through magazines together, Kat and Mary immersed themselves in playing with the kids and Karma. Karma was gentle with them, even as they tried to pull her ears off. Jude watched with pride, I watched with envy.

"How do you do it man, how do you raise kids in this world and not live in a constant state of panic and fear?"

"Who says I'm not in a constant state of panic and fear? I'm just trying to raise people who will leave the world better than they found it and praying I don't mess them up too bad in the process."

It had started the first morning I woke up with Kat and Karma under one blanket. Then Kat pulled up an app on her phone and uploaded pictures of us both to see what our kids might look like. I fell in love with every fabricated face. Watching her on the floor with Karma and Jude's two little ones, I gave up fighting it and just admitted to myself that I wanted kids with Kat. Reality came crashing into that dream when the twins went into a full double meltdown and Kat cut her eyes over to me; I could tell she was thinking 'aren't you glad we don't have kids!'

I met Kat at Nana's that Thanksgiving, she was waist deep in flour and grease with one of Nana's aprons on, one I knew to be a favorite. Every apron stain was a story Nana could tell you, a joy from her life tattooed into the fabric. There was not a trace of concern on Kat's face when I arrived and after a quick smooch she was back with Nana, Mom, and my aunt – passing plates, stirring pots, and gossiping.

Aside from Karma, it was just the aunts and uncles, me, Peter, and Kat that year. I stepped over the child-gate meant to keep Karma away from the cooking food and found a seat with a pleasant view of the kitchen. Nana did her best to pass on all her culinary secrets and Kat gave her every bit as much attention as I had seen her give to her schooling. Karma took a seat beside me and caught Kat's eye. She gave us a quick smile and a wink, then she was right back to her studies.

After the meal Nana pulled out an old photo album to show Kat pictures of me as a kid. One that caught Kat's eye was of me as a toddler in their backyard. I was blowing the seeds off dandelions.

"Look how sweet you were!"

Nana gave a big smile as she ran her hand over the photo.

"He was the sweetest boy. Now he better be the sweetest man, or I'll jerk a knot in his tail for ya Katherine!"

"You and Liz raised a good one Nana, but I'll let ya know if he starts getting out of line."

We stayed to help clean up, but Kat had to get back home that night. With a parting kiss, she got in her car, and I got in my van. I turned the key and couldn't get over feeling like I was going home incomplete. As I was backing out, Nana came to her door, howling into the night,

"Laawd! She said wait for me daddy!"

Karma came running for the van and I popped the recently

repaired auto-sliding door open for her while Nana laughed at me. She waved and hollered her love as we started pulling down the driveway. My thoughts drifted into worry, but looking back at my Nana, she seemed fine. She blew us a kiss and shouted out again.

"You take good care o' those girls Sweetpea! I love you all!"

The folk's place was on the way, so I thought we would drop in for a minute. I pulled in and let Karma out. We got to the door, and I could hear them yelling through it. I almost knocked, but quietly let the storm door close. I knew they'd be oblivious to our presence.

We got back to the apartment and climbed up the rusting stairs to our roach infested apartment. I didn't even bother walking all the way to bed. My phone chimed with a message from Kat:

I love you

She had sent three red hearts behind the message. They weren't much, but they brought her into the room with me, which warmed the air and settled my mind. I replied, with all our love and my own three hearts.

We had decided to have a staycation between Christmas and New Year. She was off work and wouldn't have school to attend. With one holiday season under my belt, I knew there was no point in being open during that time and the most reasonable thing to do seemed like nothing.

On Christmas Eve morning we took Karma to see Nana. Grace was out in the yard when we got there and she and Karma said their hellos. Nana came out to meet us in the driveway; she was quiet, concerned I think. Kat immediately started chatting her up and she perked up, but she wasn't herself. When Kat took Karma and Grace to walk in the field, Nana spoke up.

"Did Lizzie tell you what the doctors said?"

"Yeah Nana, I'm sorry to hear it, but you're tough, you'll be alright."

"Tough times make tough people, an' time gets aroun' to us all Sweetpea, I just hate that everyone is so worried about it."

"Is there anything I can do for you while I'm here Nana?"

"I ain't dead yet Sweetpea, you gonna be just like the rest of 'em? Your uncle's been trying to get me to listen to some song about livin' like you're dying." she scoffed.

"I know that song, it's pretty good."

"Ain't nuthin' good about living like there ain't no consequences to your actions!"

"Sorry Nana, just tryin' to help, I'm sure he was too."

She glanced down and away.

"No, I'm sorry sweetpea. I can deal with a shaky hand and bag of pills, but I'm just so scared of losing all the memories of your Grandpap an' our family, and-"

She started to choke up a little and I gave her a hug. We made our way to her table, safe from all that fear.

"Your Karma sure looks happy out there, when are you gonna marry her mama?"

"…I don't know Nana. One day, I hope."

She got up and walked away without a word. I heard her rummaging around in her room and then she came back.

"I have a Christmas present for you, something Santa left a long time ago."

She held it close to her heart and it was wrapped in her shaking hands. No bows, no ribbons, no card. Her hair shined silver in the sunlight from the window. She looked like she was praying under a halo.

When she opened her hands, she held out a tiny silver ring with a faint chip of a diamond mounted on it.

"Your Grandpap gave me this as a promise. A promise to love me my whole life long. I want you to have it now."

"Nana!?"

"No, no! you take it. I haven't worn it since I met Arthur."

"Arthur?!"

"Yeah, Arthur-itis. …I don't know how much longer I'll be making my own decisions, but while I can, I've made this one."

I looked out into the yard at Kat sitting in the sparse winter grass, hugging Grace and Karma, and I took the ring from Nana's hands.

"Thank you, Nana. Is this Grandpap's silver ring you bet me?"

"It is."

"It's funny, I lost our bet, and I got the ring anyway…"

"I know my family and I knew you wouldn't find what you were looking for out there, Sweetpea. My ring was never in danger. And I know that it's not now neither."

"I'll make a good life Nana, I promise."

"Take care of these girls, baby. You take good care of them for me."

"I will Nana, I'll do my best."

Kat and Karma came back from the cold, Nana and I acted like nothing out of the ordinary had happened.

She leaned over to let Karma kiss her hand and whispered,

"And you take care of my Sweetpea!"

She stood in the door as we left, waving and shouting she loved us, but then called Grace and turned back inside. As we pulled away, I couldn't help but notice she was missing from the rearview and those few grams of silver in my pocket felt like a ton.

Kat left us for a while to celebrate with her family. When Karma and I got to the folks' she flew out of the car and up the steps to the door. She was briefly disappointed that Kat wasn't there, but once she saw presents wrapped under the tree, she knew what day it was.

Kat showed up later, a little tired from her own Christmas festivities, but no less ready to be a part of ours. That whole night, Nana's ring called to my hands from my pocket. Sitting there watching our family have Christmas, it was all I could do not to drop to the floor and beg for Kat's hand.

We made it out of there without a proposal and went home. Then we put on our most comfortable pants and the tacky sweaters we'd bought each other for the occasion. We sat down on the couch with Karma and let her open the cheap little gifts we'd bought for each other and her. The ring found a home in my sock drawer and for seven days we sat on the couch and streamed cooking shows and classic TV. Karma drooled as if she could smell the food that flashed across the screen, Kat observed that food was clearly Karma's love language and hinted that it was also her own.

When the new year came, we found ourselves watching Rod Serling guide us through the halls of his imagination in flickering black-and-white. The last thing I remember from that night was an episode about a teacher that was losing the job he loved. There was a quote from Horace Mann.

'Be ashamed to die until you have won some victory for humanity.'

With every perfect thing asleep, I wondered what – if any –

victories I had won for humanity, or what victories I might yet win. What had I done to deserve this white-haired pup, enriching my life daily, this dark-haired woman, learning to help people in the toughest struggles of their lives. Surrounded by all this beauty and love, there I was… selling junk.

When I woke up, Karma was sitting at Kat's feet by the stove and breakfast was filling the house with the smells of simmering bacon and baking biscuits. Kat smiled as she saw me rise and stepped away from the burners to give me the first kiss of that new year.

"Happy new year mister."

"Happy new year baby."

And then, someone hit fast-forward.

Daylight became a thief, sneaking in through the window every morning to steal my heart. All I wanted to do was linger in those moments that I shared with Kat and Karma on our couch, but they seemed to flash by like trees and signs on the side of the highway. I couldn't find a mountain, an object that stayed in view and slowly crept by no matter how fast life went.

The more successful the shop became, the more of a bore and struggle I found it. I'd always had trouble connecting with people, but I started noticing there were distinct types of couples that came through and given where I was at in my life, I came out of my shell with them a little bit.

Every pair came in together, maybe one would hold the door for the other, maybe they were holding hands, maybe not. Some couples, Karma would greet and trot along with them both together through a lap of the mall. Others would split up when they came in and Karma would patrol from one to the other, making sure they each had everything they needed. A third type, Karma's favorite, would go their separate ways when they came in, but spend their whole visit chasing back and forth after each other to report what treasures they had found. Karma loved them the most because they kept her busy, constantly leading them back to each other.

I wondered how they'd gotten where they were, so I just started asking. The answers I got were as varied as the products on my shelves.

"We never go to bed on an argument." Some would say.

"We always give each other space." Said others.

"We're just so similar…"

"We are so completely different…"

"We never judge each other…"

"We always tell each other when we're wrong…"

On and on the answers varied. The only thing every answer had in common was the word 'we'. They were just together, in everything in life.

I'd never thought about why I loved Kat when we were young, I just knew that I did and that was all I needed to know. As we grew up a little and started thinking more about life, it seemed like there really wasn't a reason and everything became a tallying of differences against similarities. Standing behind that counter, talking to all those old lovebirds, I knew that I loved Kat, and felt like that was all I needed to know.

As the snowbirds stopped passing through, I started noticing another type of customer. The lonely souls. Wandering my floor in silent reflection and rumination. The people that shuffled in with a grim hello and spent hours patrolling the aisles, picking up anything that brought back a memory of their life, of being alive. They made up the lion's share of my paying customers and I had never noticed.

Some had gotten used to it and had an air of contentment about them, others took their disappointments out on the world. They all started their sentences with "I" and all of them – when compared to the others – seemed sad.

By the end of Spring, I wasn't interested in balance sheets and bank accounts. All my thoughts were on these relationships I was watching, and how Kat and I compared.

We left Karma behind again around my birthday. With school consuming Kat and the shop consuming me, she felt like time away would do us both good. It was a weekend in Memphis for a festival. From the tragic look on Karma's face, you would have thought we were abandoning her in a ditch, not grandparents' house.

I had gotten a new camera and Kat had gotten a new phone. We didn't talk much, and when we did, it was talk of shop and school, Karma, and Nana, and any real conversation or connection seemed to instantly give way to the idea of vacation, the thought that all the worries and troubles of home should be left there. I mostly took pictures and she mostly scrolled her phone. It was almost like we were two strangers who just ended up in the same tour group.

They say every man gets his fill of home. Apparently, every home gets it's fill of a man too. I got the camera out when we got close to home and was going to snap a picture of Karma barreling out the door at Kat. As soon as she saw the camera, she sat down and struck a defiant pose, ears pinned back looking off at the horizon., then right before the shutter clicked, she turned up her nose and marched inside.

"She's mad at us, babe!" Kat laughed.

"We'll take her next time; she'll get over it."

"We'll see."

On the morning of Karma's 8th birthday, I sat in bed with

her, reflecting on everything we'd seen and how it all seemed like a dream I'd had the night before. There were people in that very moment trying to figure out how to launch rockets into space then land them on ships in the ocean; I was struggling to figure out who I even was. I'd missed my usual birthday visit to Nana's, so I decided to ditch the store for the day and go see her. She was inside and sang out when I knocked on the door.

"Well, what have I done for this pleasant surprise!?"

"Good morning, Nana, we just thought we'd take advantage of running our own business an come see you today."

"Is everything alright Sweetpea, you look tired."

"I am Nana… I am tired."

"You're awful young to be gettin' tired son, is the store wearing you down?"

"It's just life, Nana, I'm getting old I guess."

"Well, Sweetpea, that's what life does. It wears us down. You just gotta keep tryin' and believin'."

I looked at the shaking hands she was slowly losing control of and the gentle smile she still managed to keep on her face, and I felt a fool. I remembered that day, near a decade gone, that I was over there bawling in her arms over hearing Kat was getting married. And there I was, with Kat back in my life. I remembered her telling me that dogs have a way with broken hearts, and there I was, with Karma by my side. And here I was, worried and tired. I felt a fool. But I felt those other things too.

I shook it off and got up to refill my coffee. Karma followed me off the love seat we'd been sharing with Nana. As she leapt, she found her legs weren't as spry as they used to be and let out a little yelp as she tumbled to the ground. Nana was quick to comfort her,

"It's alright sweetie, old Arthur's a friend a'mine too."

Chapter Fourteen

Kat didn't make it up much that year. We spent what time we shared watching obscure TV shows on DVDs I'd brought up from the shop. We remembered sitting at our grandmother's houses after school watching reruns, we laughed here and there. A time or two we teared up. We talked about things we missed from our youth, then one day Mom called and gave us something else to miss.

"We're doing Thanksgiving a little different this year, Nana's been having trouble in the kitchen."

"I noticed that last time I saw her."

"And while we're on the subject, I'm probably moving in with her after new year, she's going to need help."

"Oh… Are we still having it at her place?"

"Yes, but we're all going to bring dishes instead of cooking there. Can you and Kat bring something?"

"I'll ask, but I'm sure we can."

"And I hate to ask… but can Karma sit this one out? Nana has been stumbling with Grace and we just want to keep it calm this year."

"I'm sure she'll understand."

When Thanksgiving came, Kat had everything ready to go in heat-retaining containers.

"Okay, I think I'm about ready. We'll wait to put the buns

in the oven so we can walk in smelling festive – and so you don't eat them - and when they're done, we'll go."

"I'm about ready to put a bun in your oven…"

"I need to get ready still, we have to wait until… wait… what did you say!?"

The shocked confusion on her face was priceless.

"I said I'm about ready to put a bun in your oven."

She flashed a coy smile before her posture became more playful.

"Are you telling me you wanna make a baby right now?"

She put on her best attorney face as she approached the kitchen island I'd installed and leaned over it like a courtroom bench.

"I'm tellin' you I wanna make our baby… not necessarily right now, but I'd be up for some practice."

She turned away and took a step back toward the stove.

"Well mister, some things would have to happen if we're going to have a baby. Some of those things we'll have to work for and some we'll just have to wait for-"

She turned her head to the side without moving her body and looked at me from the very corners of her eyes.

"In the meantime, we can definitely keep practicing."

I stepped around the island and she grabbed Nana's wooden spoon off the stove and tapped it on the counter like a gavel.

"BALIFF! BALIFF! Restrain this witness! Order in the court, order in the court!"

A chase ensued and turned into a tickle war on the, finally, roach free floor. Karma never left the oven window.

The timer on Kat's phone went off a moment later and it was like flipping the fun switch off.

"BUNS! HAIR! MAKEUP! Move it mister!"

With a kiss, she was gone.

I watched her do her makeup while the buns baked. It was one of my favorite pastimes, like watching an artist paint. I was about to tell her how enchanting her eyes were when the timer for the buns went off.

"Go! Go! Go!" she said in a playful tone "get them out of the oven and in the-

"In the blue bag on top of the slow cooker? I got you baby."

She finished her daily masterpiece and joined me in the kitchen.

"Take this… that goes in the back… this goes with it. You carry the blue bag and hold it for us on the way. We love you Karma, be a good girl and we'll bring you leftovers!"

Karma sat by the door peeking out through the crack until it was shut. Something about the heat of that blue bag on my lap reminded me of her when she was pup and fit in my lap. I felt bad leaving her behind.

Our meal filled our bellies, but not so much our hearts. The smells of herbs and spices that normally greeted us for Thanksgiving had been replaced by the ordinary odors of everyday life and the sound of the microwave re-heating plate after plate. Nana was sad, I think she felt like it was because of her we couldn't have a party and I'm not sure anyone told her that nothing could have been further from the truth. She was our party. Kat felt it too.

"You mom is doing a really good job with Nana."

"I'm proud of her. I worry what I'm going to do when it's my turn."

"You've got time babe, you'll figure it out."

Kat had always said the only video games she'd play were

80's games. A small console with lots of vintage games preinstalled had come out that year and was impossible to find. I scoured every place that sold them for miles and finally found one. I never saw Kat so surprised or excited about something as she was when she opened it. She kicked my tail at every game we played, despite my best efforts and years of experience. I think I always felt like she was better than me, that just proved it.

When our thumbs wore out, we all three cuddled into a ball on the couch and watched Perry Mason draw confessions from every witness that took the stand. Dad had always loved that show and it was the last thing we watched before bedtime growing up. Kat had never seen it, so when a box set came through the shop right before the holidays, I basically demanded we spend staycation catching her up. Karma didn't demand much of our attention, she just sat with us and fell into the leisurely nostalgic rhythm of that week.

Closing the shop had been on my mind. When Karma took her last break one night and tumbled down the last half of our cheese grater staircase after a big winter storm laid down over a foot of snow, I made up my mind.

All the snow broke her fall, but the steps banged her up. I consoled her and made sure she wasn't seriously hurt, then I carried her back up the stairs and walked my little town alone, camera in tow. It was desolate. The roads were impassable, everything was quiet and bright, the only sounds to be heard were the faint clicks of the blinking traffic lights and the occasional breeze rustling the frozen limbs of the trees. Everything was glowing in the reflection of the streetlights off the unbroken blanket of snow. It was beautiful, like the clock had been turned back to simpler days, when the world took time to sleep. I walked the town until dawn trying to preserve that stillness.

Karma limped for the better part of a week but seemed to be okay overall. I called up the property owner to let him know I wouldn't be renewing my lease in the spring and started paying more attention to Karma after that; watching her move, remembering how she used to jump and twirl, trying to remember the last time I'd seen her do that. They say one year of a human's life is like seven to a dog. One night while tallying up the shop's books I went over to the side of my spreadsheet and did the math, my 'little girl' was about to be sixty-three. It's so unfair, I thought to myself, so unfair that such a happy creature should grow old so fast.

I put everything I owned on sale, put all my booth owners on notice and contracted Dad to do a going out of business auction. By the time it was all said and done, I still had over half what was in my shop – some of it was mine, some of it was Nana's, some of it was my aunt's and uncle's, and all of it had no place to go. We worked it out, improvised a plan C, and on the last day in that old donut shop, my castle in the middle of my small town, the building was empty. Dad's garage was full, and my faithful Rodeo, which I'd never had the time to fix nor the heart to sell, was buried under a mountain of other people's memories.

We found good company with Dad, now living alone in my great grandmother's old house with two cats that weren't his. Most of his breakfast club was in the hospital or the ground, and he'd recently heard that their favorite restaurant was closing. His house, which had once been so full and clean, now held only the remnants of his family and bore the scars and pungent smells of all the pets that had passed through.

Karma was happy. Karma was always happy to be wherever she found herself it seemed, so long as she was around people she could love and make smile. Her reunion with the cats was exciting for her. Just like old friends meeting after years apart, they picked up where they left off, Nubs cuddling up next to her on the couch, Solly hissing and clawing at her approach. Karma made herself at home, like everything was just as it should be.

We had her 9th birthday party at Nana's. Mom was always the driving force behind that tradition, and while Karma was her birthday princess self, ripping at presents and soaking up attention, I was missing people for her. Dad wasn't there and Peter and Kat couldn't make it. I wondered if she understood the troubles people have, how the forces that drive people forward in life often drive them apart.

The last story on the nightly news when we got home was headlined, 'The last VCR has been made.' I had five of them in the garage, leftovers from the shop, but it was still a watershed moment. All the home movies we had made as kids, all the Birthdays, Christmases, and Thanksgivings that were captured on tape, all were dependent on that little black box to be played. And now, they weren't making them anymore.

The news finished its broadcast and Karma came trotting into the room. She found her place on the bed she had re-stolen from Solly and settled into what had become her favorite thing – watching Perry Mason with Dad.

Solly made his way to his usual bed, Dad's lap. Nubs made her way to her perch on the back of the couch and every shining eye turned to the monochrome legal drama the accounted for the last hour of every weekday. Dad had watched it our whole life and had seen every episode. Perry always won. However rough our day had been, Perry always found a way to win at the end.

The further Kat had gotten in school, the less I was seeing her and the more she and Dad had found themselves at odds on finer points of Law. We spent most of our time together at her place, without Karma.

The first big fight I remember us having, at least for that chapter of our lives together, was during a spring snowstorm. It was less massive than the winter storm that tried to kill Karma, but being snowed in for a week was still fresh on everyone's mind. It blew in one night while I was at her place and - for reasons I can't remember - I felt like I needed to get home, even though there was already several inches down. Kat was afraid for me and didn't want to be left alone. She cried for me not to go out into that mess, but I wouldn't listen. I told her I didn't want to get stuck away from Karma, and that was true enough, but I think the real truth was that her place didn't feel like home, and If I was going to be stuck somewhere, I wanted it to be home. Whatever my reason, things were never quite the same after that. I guess we'd been growing apart for a while, but after that fight, it was like the flood gates opened on all the unspoken tensions between us.

On one of her few visits to see us at home, we had a huge fight about time together. Every time I looked down at Karma, her expression asked me how I could treat her mommy that way. Kat rested her case with:

"It's never enough for you Mark, nothing is ever enough!"

Judge Karma ruled decidedly in favor of Kat.

After closing the shop, I took a job at a customer service call center, back to the same kind of work that ultimately led to meeting Kat. Five days a week I filled my Grandpap's thermos and drove a half hour each way in traffic to deal with eight-to-ten hours of problems people had with their orders. It felt like everyone in the world was upset. Nana saw my troubles when I visited her.

"Penny for your thoughts?"

"Nana, I'll pay you a dollar to take'em off my mind."

She looked scared before she asked.

"Is it you and Katherine?"

"I'm afraid that's part of it, Nana…"

She rang her trembling hands together.

"Ohh Sweetpea… I pray God tie a knot 'tween you two that the Devil can't never undo!'

"I just worry we're not compatible anymore Nana or wonder if we ever even were. I feel like I don't make her happy and like she's never there, even when we're together. It's like we're becoming strangers. Sometimes… I feel like the best thing I could do for us both is to just grab Karma get back on the road."

"Child… love ain't about compatible. Love's about compassion and patience, about forgiveness and havin' faith in what your heart tells ya. When we met, your Grandpap and me was kids and didn't have no idea who we was or was gonna be. We went through being lots'a different people on our way to being your Nana and Grandpap."

She paused and a somber smile crept over her face.

"Your Grandpap and me had lots'a days thinkin' we'd made a mistake, that maybe there was somebody better out there for us, but we never gave up on our hearts, even when our heads gave up on everythin' else… I think our hearts was right! You've just gotta listen to your heart Sweetpea!"

"And your dog?" I smiled.

"And your dog!! Even now, my heart ain't give up on your

Grandpap and I know his ain't give up on mine. You gotta remember baby, Katherine's a human too, with her own thoughts and feelin's and tribulations to work through. Sometimes love means stayin', even when you don't wanna be there and they don't want ya there."

"I think the world would argue with you Nana."

"If all them hippie ideas 'bout love was true, the world wouldn't be so broke all to pieces and gettin' meaner every day."

"You're probably right."

"You and Katherine have it rougher'n we did, you got that ol' internet and all these people tellin' ya a hundred different things. Listen to your heart child."

"I do love her, I always have... I just don't feel like she sees it or cares anymore… What am I gonna do, Nana? What am I gonna do…"

"You gotta talk about your feelin's together, Sweetpea. It's hard cause feelin's take control of us and most folk like to think they're always in control. Just talk to her baby and listen when she talks to you."

"I love you, Nana!"

She took my hand in hers.

"I love you too, Sweetpea… Now there's been a time or two I didn't love your ways, and there may still be more, but I always have and always will love you. Think about that with Katherine…" she said as she squeezed my hand and smiled "…think about her."

Nana knew another knot had been undone. As Peter and I had suspected, there was more to Mom moving in with Nana than just helping Nana. She and Dad had decided they had separate ways to go. They stayed friends, we stayed a family, and nothing really changed.

Kat joined us for the last game of the World Series that year. Dad was obsessed because the Cubs were set to win, and our family had always rooted for the underdogs. Dad went to get burgers for everyone, came back and handed out our meals, but in his obsession with the game he made a fatal error. He sat his hamburger on the coffee table and turned his attention to the screen.

Kat and I were eyeing Karma, knowing what was going through her mind. We heard the crack of a ball against a bat and looked up to watch a player run to first. When we looked back, the burger was gone.

Dad was oblivious to the crime, but Karma knew what she'd done. She sat there looking at Dad with shame and remorse in her eyes, even as she was chewing the last bits of his dinner. Without looking, he reached for his meal and found only an empty void. Me and Kat filled that void with laughter. It sounded like it was coming from the TV or a neighbor's house.

Despite her thieving ways, Karma got two Thanksgivings and two Christmases that year, one at Nana's and one at Dad's. As awkward as it was for us, the humans, she loved every minute of it all. After Christmas at Dads, Kat and I abandoned my little girl with him for the week. We'd decided to have our annual staycation at her place that year, mainly because I no longer had a place really. Unfortunately, her apartments were one of those with dog breed restrictions and Karmas were on the list.

I was missing my pup as soon as we got there, but there were other things that dampened that week too. Kat's balcony overlooked a residential neighborhood, one of the houses had this big fenced in yard with a Shepherd living out his days behind chain-link. At first, he just made me miss Karma. Then, I started thinking about how much those people had probably wanted that dog when they got it, and how now he seemed to have become another yard ornament with the rusting swing set and moldy birdbath. I felt sorry for the little guy, his loneliness a consequence of someone else's pursuit of happiness and yet his happiness to see them never dulled. As the days of our staycation passed, I grew proud of the little guy for his ability to love without needing to be loved back.

Kat and I tried to talk about spending more time together, she went on about all the classes, groups, and things she had to keep up with. She said she felt like she was always behind. I tried to understand, we didn't fight, but I made it my new year's resolution to just accept that things weren't going to change.

Change in another part of my life crept over the horizon with phone call. Ben and his girl had split, his sprawling ranch was just an empty house now and worth about three times what he'd paid. Never without a goal, he was looking at taking a job in Virginia. The clearance process for it was long and he was hoping to spend the in-between time around here, specifically to be closer to Nana.

I pulled Dad aside that night to clear everything with him, he was more than happy to add another member to our lonely-hearts club and with one more phone call, we had a new roommate on the way.

"… so long as you don't mind rooming with two old men, two cats and a Karma."

Change was on the horizon for Peter too. He was moving out of his cottage and into the old timer's farmhouse. The old couple wanted to get closer to town and doctors, but the guy just couldn't bring himself to sell the farm yet. He worked out a deal with Peter to take over daily operations in a rent-to-own setup.

Me and Dad went out to see him one afternoon in the early spring, he had done a respectable job updating everything and preparing for his new roommate. Rose – the cute girl Karma fished out of that crowd for him in Texas - was moving up sometime that year. Dad surveyed the place and saw his own father's farm in the stock and the crops.

"Looks good son, looks real good."

"Thanks Pops. I'm surprised how complicated it's been to build a simple life."

"What are you gonna do with the cottage?"

"I think I'm gonna try to rent that out as a B&B."

Somehow those letters made an unrelated connection in Dad's brain.

"That reminds me; Mark, have you noticed those things that feel like BBs on Karma's belly?"

Chapter Fifteen

I had been living like a normal person. Spending 10-12 hours a day away from home and doing my best to be available when it was convenient for Kat. I hadn't paid that much attention to Karma.

Dad was right, it felt like little packs of BB gun ammo in her skin. She was overdue for a checkup anyway, so I called to schedule an appointment with Doc. Peter had checked her out and thought it might be a little infection, so I was completely unconcerned when we got to the vet. Karma was happy to see everyone, especially the fifty-pound cat that thundered around that place. I figured we were just going to be in-and-out with some kind of treatment for her and maybe an update on the fatty tumors she'd developed.

Doc's face shattered that illusion. He didn't say anything and didn't really give anything away in his motions or actions. It was just a fraction of a second in his eyes while he was checking her out and I knew something was wrong. He looked me straight in the eyes and began.

"It's not good. I would be willing to bet that's cancer of the mammary gland – in simplest terms breast cancer – and we need to get all that out of there."

He stood with genuine concern for this pup he had nursed back from deaths door a decade before. While we both took our deep breaths, the little pup in the middle had no clue what was going on and was happy to be with her daddy and her Doc.

"We could biopsy them to be sure, but I want to get those out of there Mark. We need to do some blood work to make sure she can survive surgery and I need you to understand that it is going to be a significant operation."

"How significant?"

He had Karma play dead for us and started with his finger under her front leg, then traced a line all the way down her belly, almost to where her back legs met.

"We're gonna have to cut that whole mammary chain out, she'll be under for several hours."

"What about recovery?"

"We'll have you keep her sedated that first week, if she tore her stitches, it could get bad. While we've got her under, I think we should go ahead and get these fatty tumors off as well, they feel a little firmer than last time."

I was shell shocked. Karma just thought Doc was playing with her the whole time. A tech came in to draw blood and they said they would call when the results came back. I was mortified and promised Karma we'd never play dead again.

The waiting to hear back was awful. Every time the phone made a sound, my heart stopped. Telling the folks was awful, and my birthday, which was that same week, was awful. Kat was out of town, Karma had cancer, the folks were barely speaking to each other, and Nana was starting to act different on a new Parkinson's medication. Welcome to 35.

The vet finally called and said Karma was clear for surgery and that they had availabilities the week of her birthday, I asked if we could do it the day after her birthday. I just wanted to be sure we got that one more party with her, for her.

Everyone came to Dad's for Karma's 10th birthday. Mom

came, Kat came, Peter came – everyone sat their own lives aside and celebrated that day for my little girl. None of us said it, but we were all scared. Kat stayed the night and we sat up most of it just holding Karma between us, rubbing her belly, knowing she was about to be cut from neck to tail.

Kat walked us to the van the next morning and helped Karma up into the passenger seat. She gave her a long hug and a kiss on her head. When she reached for my hand, hers was trembling. I kissed it and she smiled. Then she stepped away from the window and told Karma everything was going to be okay. When I found Kat in the rearview, the morning Sun was glinting in her tears.

I walked Karma into the vet and handed her off to a tech who told me,

"We'll keep you posted; it will be later this evening before we're done."

I spent that entire day trying not to be afraid, trying to believe in Karma, in her magic. I tried to believe everything was going to be okay. It wasn't like parvo, when I felt sorry for her. This was different, I felt sorry for her and I was afraid the pin that held my whole life together might get pulled out. The phone rang earlier than I expected and it felt like a knife in my heart. I bit my tongue and accepted the call.

"She did great Mark; she is waking up now. We want to keep her here the rest of the day, but you can come pick her up about an hour before we close."

My baby was butchered. She staggered around the corner, glassy eyed, with a big stitched up gash on her arm, two on her back, and a seam all the way down her underside – it looked like staples and strings were all that was holding her together. She could barely stand up from the pain and sedation, but she managed to wag her tail when she saw me.

We laid her over on a blanket and hoisted her into the van, when I got to her home, everyone was waiting. Peter helped me get her out and into the house, but once we got in the door, she was determined to walk and show everyone she was okay. She staggered around the living room like a village drunk. Mom and Kat smiled and cried. Dad and me and Peter couldn't help laughing at her stumbling around, licking anyone within tongue's reach. We herded her back to my room and she collapsed onto her bed, where the family huddled around her until the sedatives dragged her back to sleep.

We all took our turns taking care of Karma. Kat was there daily, helping change out puppy pads and keeping Karma's wounds clean. She was better than me about seeing that Karma was uncomfortable and needed help rolling over onto her other side. Karma seemed almost ashamed, like she was a burden or maybe like the pain was punishment for something she'd done wrong. That was the hardest part of it all, I wanted so badly for her to understand that sometime healing means hurting.

After she got her stitches out, Kat came up to treat her to a pup cup from the local ice cream shop. She had a little pink ribbon that she pinned on Karma's collar for the ride. We pulled in the drive-thru with Karma's head jammed out Kat's back window and ordered our milkshakes and Karma's pup cup. As soon as her tongue hit the frozen whipped cream in that cup, Karma's eyes bulged out of her head like she was a cartoon. She licked and licked and licked until she was sure there was nothing left in that cup, and then she ate the cup. Kat and I slowly slurped our shakes and remembered being kids, unspoiled by life and unafraid to hope. Ice cream takes you back like that.

We enjoyed it so much, we decided to set another ice cream date for the upcoming eclipse. Standing there in the shadow of the moon, all the birds and bugs went silent; it felt like the everything stopped, and all around there was a stillness and peace, as if the world was taking a deep breath. The universe spun around, and a crescent sun smiled down on us. The passing of the shadow kindled hope that the darkness in my own life might pass with it.

No sooner than we got Karma on her feet, Ben moved in, and Nana fell. She was doing something with Grace and lost her balance, breaking her collar bone and badly twisting her ankle. Kat was still out of school and volunteered to help Mom look after her. There was a debate about what to do with Grace until Dad volunteered to bring her to our place. Unfortunately, he forgot to check with Karma.

We got Grace moved in. She and Karma knew each other, but in their age, they had both gotten a little snippy. We just kept them separated at first, until they set their own boundaries. Mom made frequent trips over to see her girls, give them both treats, and to walk with Grace.

Grace loved it outside and preferred to be on a lead in the yard over being under any roof. We had her anchored so she could come three feet in the back door for us to hook and unhook her without having to put our shoes on.

One day, Mom called Grace to the door for a treat and Karma ran through the house to get in line for hers. I like to believe Karma lunged for the treat, but I would forgive anyone who said they saw Karma lunge for Graces throat. The result was a dogfight. Words were of no use, however long it took me to yell each of their names once was all I gave that solution. I was looking for Plan B when Ben came running. I was pulling

Karma away from Grace, Mom was pulling Grace's lead back to the door, and the girls were latched onto each other, shaking their heads trying to rip chunks out of each other. Grace lunged and pulled Mom to the ground before I managed to slide Karma back to Ben on the tile floor and grab a hold of Grace. He sprawled out, flat on top of Karma, and put her in a headlock with his free hand over her eyes.

Grace was berserk, I tried to calm her down, but she was still lunging at Karma and snapping her jaws. I sharpened my tone and tried to pivot us away from Karma's snarling breath. Ben looked like he had Karma pinned and Mom had regained her feet. She was at the door waving me over, too distraught to speak. I loosened my grip on Grace to turn her around toward the door but in her frenzy, she snapped at my face. Her fang caught the inside of my nose, and I yelled out in pain.

Karma went into a rage and stood up with Ben's full weight on her back. She turned and started marching toward Grace, furiously grunting with every step, carrying Ben as she went. Grace completely gave up and fled for the door. Ben chuckled and got Karma's feet back out from under her, Mom got the back door latched, then Ben carried Karma to my room and shut the door.

We noticed the blood when he came back through the kitchen. It was all over that place. We looked each other over, Ben had a drop or two, I had a soggy spot, and it wasn't mine. We bolted outside to find Mom in tears and Grace in what looked like a state of shock. She was bleeding in several places and her back leg was ripped open. Ben flew into action, taking his own shirt off and pressuring the wound with it. Then, just as calm as if he were reading a recipe out of a book, he started giving orders.

"Aunt Liz, get a blanket from the living room. Cuz, get her

back seat down and lay some towels over it. What time is it?"

"Uhhh… 3:30"

"Cuz, call the vet once the car is ready and tell them what you see here."

I ran to the bathroom for towels, then back out to Mom's car and got the doors open. I couldn't get her back seat to lay down and was tugging and pulling on it when I slipped in the gravel. Fury consumed me. I jumped to my feet taking 5 or 6 good shots at the mailbox before kicking it off its mount, losing my footing in the process, and falling right back to gravel where I started. I froze in overwhelm until I heard Ben call me from the back yard and ran around the house.

"Help me lift her."

"Mom, I can't get your seat down, and I haven't called the vet."

"She's gotta keep pressure on that wound while we carry her, we'll deal with the rest at the car."

Ben took over pressure at the car and Mom got her seat down. We let pressure off for a moment to get Grace loaded and swap Ben's shirt for a towel.

"Aunt Liz, you go around and sit in the back to keep pressure on this. Call the vet and I'll drive."

As Mom stepped away, Ben whispered,

"It's not bleeding as much as I'd expect and she's not really moving, I don't know what's going on, but if it was a person, I'd say it's bad. Stay here and clean that mess up before your Pops gets home; I'll call if we need a hole dug."

Luckily, the wound on her leg wasn't as bad as it looked. They didn't even stitch it; the shock and thin blood was old age and over-exertion they thought. While they had her, they noticed a growth on her neck and said they wanted to biopsy it. Then, home ran like a hospital again – Grace was in wound care; Karma was on behavioral evaluation. Mom was terrified to come over and the cats paid the whole thing no mind whatsoever.

With everything that had been going on - especially with Nana's fall - Kat had been right there, just like part of the family, helping anywhere she could. It was her that told me Thanksgiving was cancelled that year. There had always been food on Nana's table that Thursday in November, for as long as any of her kids, grandkids, and great grandkids had been alive. I understood, but it broke my heart. I was as sad for Nana as I was for myself and the rest of us. Everyone was going to stop in and see her that weekend, but I knew that just wouldn't make up for missing all the things that went into her one night with her family around her table. Kat had taken the liberty of arranging our visit for Thursday night.

"I told your mom we would make something and bring it over, I hope that's okay."

"That sounds great baby, I don't know what we'd do without you."

She made everything and packed it up from her place. Nana's ring found its way into my hand while I waited for her that night, as I sat thinking how she had said I wouldn't find my heart out on the road, I wondered if she had been thinking of Kat, if somehow she knew. I looked back at the year that had passed, and how Kat had been there every step of the way, through every struggle, just like one of us. I really couldn't imagine what I would do without her, and I got really scared of losing her. All the trouble and distance between us was still there, but when it mattered, Kat was right there beside us. I heard her horn beep in the driveway. The ring put itself into my pocket.

Smell is a funny thing. I'd asked Peter once how he could stand the smell of the rescue shelter; he told me he got used to it and didn't smell it anymore. Some smells are like that, others you get used to and don't miss until they are gone. When opened the door, all we could smell was disinfectant and the apple pie candle burning on her table.

Nana was ecstatic to have us and complimented everything Kat had done, thanking her over and over for being around to help. Mom got Nana her meds and when they kicked in, she helped her to bed. When Mom came back out, she went straight for Kat, in tears, and thanked her over and over for everything she had done. She walked us to the door and gave us her love as we made our way to the car. I heard the house door shut and stopped.

"Katherine…"

"Yeah babe?"

"Thank you for all the things you do for my family."

"I love your family, just like my own."

"Would you make it your own?"

She stopped.

"…Among the many things we'd need to discuss before I can answer that, a big shiny ring would be at the top of the list."

Her eyes followed my hand into my pocket and she stopped me. She was quiet, just above a whisper, but firm.

"Don't. I love you Mark, but not right now, not right here. It's hard to see what us spending the rest of our lives together looks like right now and with what's going on with Nana, I don't think this is what we should be focused on."

"I think it's exactly what we should focus on. Who else will be able to tell my kids what their Nana was like? It's not like it'd be your first walk down the aisle!"

Her eyes went cold then lit with fire.

"How dare you, Mark. I lost everything I'd worked for, not to mention a family I loved in that divorce. And do you even remember why you and I broke up in the first place? Do you remember driving your life off a cliff while your real friends helplessly watched? Do you know how bad it hurt to see you waste every opportunity you were given? Opportunities for our future! But I stayed. I stayed because I love you and couldn't bear to leave you alone in that darkness. I kept believing in you, ready to do anything I could to help you find your way out. I stayed, and what did you do?"

I had to look away.

"You betrayed me for a stranger, Mark. I know we were just kids, but to this day, that wound has never healed. To this day, we have never talked about it, and you want to stand here, in Nana's driveway, with some ring you found in your junk pile and tell me that getting married is exactly what we need to talk about right now?"

We all make mistakes. We try not to think about them. We tell ourselves stories, rationalize or make excuses, but true regrets are always there waiting for those moments when we can't lie to ourselves about the damage we've done. The fiery chill in her stare was unbearable. I slipped away into despair. I forgot about us, I forgot about love, I just hurt and hated myself for hurting her.

"I understand… I'd do anything in my power to fix us, but I can't fix the past… I'm so sorry, Katherine."

"…let's just go, we can talk about this later."

"You head on home; I'll walk back to my place…"

"Mark, get in the car-"

"It's okay, I wanna walk, I think I need to walk."

"Babe, it's not-… You know what, fine! I tried!"

I heard the empty thud of her door closing. I couldn't look, I couldn't watch her leave. I just raised my hand to wave and started walking toward the safety of the memories in my grandmother's back yard, and away from the crumbling dreams behind me. Her car made a thump as she put it in gear, the white lights coming from behind me turned to red and then, all the light was gone.

Every step home was a look back at the mistakes I'd made with her, including my most recent. By the time I arrived, I hated myself for not being better, for losing her in the first place, for being someone she couldn't see herself spending the rest of her life with, for everything. Still, I was lucky. On the other side of my front door were people who loved me unconditionally and when I opened it, Karma was right there waiting to tend my wounds. We carried my broken heart to bed; Karma carried more than her fair share. She had spoiled me, and she wasn't the only one. I expected too much from people, but I didn't see it then.

Kat called the next day. Hurt and fear boiled into anger and rage, we both said things that shouldn't have been said and should never be repeated. All we could agree on was that we were unhappy. The last thing I remember saying was that I hoped she'd keep visiting Nana and I thanked her for her time as coldly as a telemarketer. My heart felt like one of Karma's chew toys.

It started the next night. The haunting. Every night, she was there in my dreams and I would awake to the feeling that she was hiding and I had to find her. Every morning, reminding myself she was gone, and why. Always noticing all the places she was missing from the day, all the moments made hollow without her.

Jude and I hung out a lot more in the immediate aftermath. It helped being around someone who remembered, who knew my story, who didn't have to ask me questions about it. That changed the night the news reported that the last white rhino had died, and I teared up a little at how lonely he must have been. Jude asked how I was doing with everything, and I couldn't lie to him the way I'd been lying to myself.

"I just wanted a normal life man. I just wanted her and Karma and to build a life around that."

"Have you ever felt like you were 'normal' dude?"

He made quotes in the air with his fingers as he said 'normal'.

"Honestly… no…"

"Then why try to be?"

I didn't have an answer for him, and that little hole he poked in the dam started leaking anytime I was over there. I would do well at keeping my mind forward anywhere else but being there, with them, made it hard not to miss Katherine, hard not to remember. Little by little, I stopped going over and I never told them why.

Ben had livened up Dad's place, and managing Grace and Karma gave me a good excuse to keep busy at home. Any time I felt sorry for myself, I looked at that scar running down the entirety of Karma's belly and remembered how lucky I was to have her still. And there was Grace, struggling with all her mounting issues. We weren't sure how old she was, but it was getting harder for her to get around, and the growth on her neck was an inoperable cancer. I really started focusing on helping her more than being with Karma, it seemed like Karma understood. We had Karma's annual checkup visit with Doc, he reported she looked cancer free and healthy for her age, aside from the few extra pounds she'd put on. With a clean bill of health and Ben - her dogfather - as our honored guest, we threw her a combination 11th birthday/one-year cancer free party at the house. Then, we went back to the routine our lives had become.

Chapter Sixteen

Rose had one simple demand before she would move north. There had to be cats. Nubs and Solly were never technically ours, so when Peter settled himself into his new place, the cats moved away. Ben went with them, off to his new job in Virginia, about which, he could not talk. Then there were four. Pops, Karma, Grace, and me.

We all had to adjust. Ben hadn't been there long, but we quickly missed his bellowing laughter filling the rooms. Within a few weeks, we got used to the absence of our guest. Nubs and Solly had been like wandering decor for all the years since Peter moved in over there. One day they were on the couch, the next day a countertop, another day on top of the fridge. Our eyes started playing tricks on us in their absence. A blanket left on the back of the couch would morph into Nubs. A cat fight outside would send us both running to the door to save Solly from the neighborhood bullies. They never demanded attention or needed much help; they were just quiet presences. Their quiet absence took a lot more time to get used to.

Grace was starting to seem like she might be the next departure from our house. Doc thought her cancer was spreading and she was too old to do any kind of surgery on. She was having trouble getting around and was getting stuck on the floor occasionally. Every time I helped her up, she would turn her amber eyes up at me. They looked grateful. Grace was a rescue. Even when she was at Nana's, she always seemed so grateful for attention and love, while Karma always seemed like she felt a little entitled to it.

The more we helped, the weaker Grace got. It got bad enough that she couldn't get up without us. From there, it wasn't long before she could barely walk. We all talked about putting her to sleep, but she had such a bright light in her eyes and we couldn't bring ourselves to extinguish it. Every morning, she was happy to see everyone, even Karma. Every day she would wag her tail and lick our faces when we helped her up and out the door, every day her actions assured us she wanted to be here.

One morning when I went to help Grace up, the look in her eyes started to change. The gratitude was there, but something else had crept in, a tiredness, maybe even a shame. It felt like she was telling me she was sorry for being a burden. It felt like she was giving up. That night, when we all gathered around the TV, I saw her look pleadingly at Karma like she just wanted a friend, like she just wanted another dog to be close to her. Karma got up and walked over then curled up beside her and they fell asleep there in the floor together. Dad and I were speechless. It was like a war had ended. I drained the battery on my phone taking pictures and the two of them slept there until morning.

Grace never moved far from where she was left, she couldn't. Usually that was on her bed in the kitchen, with Dad sleeping in his room, Karma in mine. We woke up one morning to find her in the hall, waiting to greet us as we started our day. I don't know how she got there, she couldn't even stand up by herself anymore, but she had done it on her own and was proud of herself for it. I felt like she just didn't want to be alone and, astonished as we were, it was heartbreaking that our doors weren't open that night.

On Mom's next visit, we knew. Grace was always excited to see Mom, no matter how rough her day had been. I was standing there when Mom came in that day. Grace looked up at us both, exhausted. All I could see in her eyes was, 'please… make it stop.'

Mom could see it too. We helped her outside and she just laid there in the sun, looking out over the grass with her chin on the ground.

"Mom… I think it's time."

Tears streamed down Mom's face as she looked down on our helpless Grace. She knew the only way to love her now was to let her go.

"I think you're right… I think Gracie is done with this fight…"

"Do you want me to call the vet?"

She could only manage to nod her head.

Nana had started getting confused and Mom knew from talking to her that she thought Grace had died already. We didn't want her to suffer that loss twice and left her out of that day. Dad and I got the car ready while Mom sat in the yard and ran her hands over Grace's brown and white fur. The three of us loaded her into the car, Mom sat in the back with Grace's head on her lap. I kissed her and told her I loved her. I told her she was a good girl, and I was happy we'd got to spend this time together. I never said goodbye.

As they pulled away, I opened the garage for a pick and a shovel, then I started digging a hole. When that grave was dug, I just fell into it until Karma scratching at the door pulled me out. I lifted myself up out of the dirt and made my way to the door. When I let her out, she just sat and looked at me until I sat down beside her, then she laid her head on my lap. I ran my hand over her scarred white fur and words just fell out of my mouth.

"Please don't make me make that decision for you Karma, please…"

I struggled against the urge to get Nana, so she could say farewell to Grace, but I knew we were doing the right thing. I got to thinking about how treasured Nana's memories had been to her, about how her disease was slowly stripping that away. She could see it happening, and now what was defining her life was the memories she'd given everyone else. The value of everything slowly deflated while I sat with Karma, waiting for Grace.

Mom and Dad pulled back into the driveway. We all three lifted Grace's lifeless body from the back and carried it to the porch. Mom brought a blanket with Grace's name embroidered on it, something Nana had made before she lost the ability to sew. Peter arrived and we all gathered around the pup that had rescued our Nana from loneliness. We remembered her. We shared our stories and our thoughts about her life, just as if she were lying in a casket at a funeral home. We mourned our Grace, just as we would have mourned anyone that we had loved and lost. Then, the four of us lifted the embroidered fleece blanket and carried her to her forever bed in Dad's back yard.

Karma aimlessly wandered the house after that. I wanted to take her to Nana's, but they were cycling through medications and had hit a bad combination. She had started asking where Grandpap was, where her own parents were. It was like everyone she'd loved and cared about had just vanished and she didn't know how or why.

She was still in rough shape by the holidays and we were all just trying to support Mom. Peter stepped up to the plate that Christmas and invited everyone to his place to eat. We had all met Rose when she moved up, but none of us really knew much about her outside of what Peter had shared. There was a much-needed excitement in the air at getting to sit around a table with her and share all our embarrassing stories about this bearded farm boy she'd moved halfway across the country for.

For the first time since Grace had passed, we were all laughing. Karma was reunited with her cat siblings, surrounded by her whole family, and more herself than I had seen her in a while. We all gathered around Peter's tree and he started handing out presents.

"And this one is for you Karma!"

She wasted no time opening the fresh cow bone Peter's butcher had prepared for her. She paid nothing else in the world any mind as she dragged it across the ancient wooden floors he had refinished, and she didn't touch another present the whole night.

We were about to open our own gifts when my phone rang. It was Mary. She was crying. I understood her words, but I couldn't connect them to their meaning. There had been a car accident. Jude was coming home. He didn't make it. The faces around that room were all fixed on mine. Confused. Concerned. In a cold, flat tone, I told them.

"Jude didn't make it home… … …Jude died."

I stood up to go outside and stumbled over Karma and her bone. Peter came outside behind me, and I collapsed. Half-forgotten memories of Jude and Mary and Kat, the thought of his fatherless children, his widowed wife, the now completely extinguished hopes that we would all be living and raising kids together. The regret over the distance I'd let come between us. It all came out in tears and one repeated word.

"No... no... no..."

Peter stood beside me in that fire.

"Do you want me to drive you to the hospital?"

"Mary said there's no point, he's gone. She's heading down with her dad and her mom is watching the kids. She said there's no point, that it's better I don't... I'm sorry man, I'm sorry... You and Rose did such a good job on everything tonight and... I'm just sorry man."

"You're all right brother, you don't have anything to be sorry for, I'm sorry you lost your best friend. We're here, this is your family... You're gonna be alright."

"I love you brother. I love you."

He held me close. He held me up.

"I love you." he said.

Our new year's party was a wake. I did what I could to help Mary with the arrangements. Tom flew in to perform the service. There was no casket to carry, all that remained of my friend was ashes in a wooden box. I was doing my best to occupy the kids and I would have given anything for the funeral home to have allowed dogs.

Both Jude's parents were there with their new spouses. The couples sat across the room from each other, mirrored images of grief and support. Jude's kids understood the facts of the loss, but it was the first death of their lives. They had no way of understanding its finality. Tom gave a eulogy that Jude would have liked. The last thing he said moved me.

"Things come and things go in this life, all we can do is cherish them while they're here and do our best to learn when to hold on, and when to let go. So many things are out of our control. Maybe our story is planned… maybe not. Either way, it's our story. The story of all of us, each a character in the story of this world. If we keep our hearts open and cherish the moments we're given, even on days like today, if we carry on through our trials together with the memory of the ones we've lost, in the company of the ones we love, then we give joy to this story, to Jude's story, and to the story we all share."

At the end of the service, we played a song Jude loved and I stood up to bring the wooden box to Mary. It was heavier than I expected, the walk back to Mary seemed longer. After I handed her the box, we sat until the song finished. The funeral director came in, thanked everyone, and told them they were dismissed. People lined up to give final condolences to Mary and I noticed Katherine in the line.

They cried in each other's arms, then Katherine came to see me. She was carrying the remnants of her eye makeup on a tissue.

"I'm sorry you lost him, Mark… I don't know what to say."

"You too…" was all I could muster.

She gave me a hug and she said goodbye. With Katherine by my side, I could face any future without fear. Without her, they were all terrifying. Before I could find another word to say, she was at the door. I went after her and caught her at her car. Mary tried to tell me not to go, it was no use. I wasn't in control.

"Kat!"

She turned with a cautious look in her eyes.

"Please come home Kat…"

"Not here Mark, please… do not do this here…"

I begged her to come back. She begged me to stop. Then, finally, I pushed her too far.

"JUST! STOP!!!... It is time to let this go Mark! It's time…

It's just time. Goodbye, Mark. I'm sorry but… just… goodbye."

She got in her car and drove away. I couldn't think. I couldn't feel. I just stood in the funeral home parking lot, another dead thing.

I started spending all my paychecks on Kentucky paint stripper. My family did their best, Karma did her best, but I couldn't even look them in the eyes. I was inconsolable. I couldn't make myself go to work. I sat in the parked van and stared, sometimes for an hour. My heart would race when I thought of Jude, or of Her, or of anything I cared about. It felt like there was battery acid in my veins and my chest was going to explode. Like I was going to die.

Within a month, I'd lost my job and started drinking my savings away. There was no escaping it. Then, the real crying started, the crippling kind, the kind that drags you to the floor and holds you down. It's not that I couldn't believe it, it's that I couldn't deny it. I had no idea how many tears I'd saved for that chapter of my life, no clue how much a person could hurt. I cried in my dreams.

I hid from Karma. I locked her out of our room. She would paw at my door and I would tell her to go away. Any time she caught me out of the room, she walked over to check on me. The best I could give her was a quick pat on her head and an order to find her Gramps.

Mary called me around Jude's birthday in the late spring. I hadn't talked to her much since the funeral. Our conversation began with silence, then I found my words.

"I'm sorry Mary, sorry I wasn't around more after… I'm sorry I put that distance between us before… I told myself I needed time. I just thought there would be more time…"

"I understand Mark, you've always run from feelings that were too strong for you. You've always made it look like you were running toward something, but you've always been running away. We missed you then, and I miss you now. You knew Jude better than anyone; you knew who he was before he met me… I want the twins to know you, to know him. None of us are guaranteed time, Mark-"

"I am so sorry Mary-"

"Mark-"

"I just can't find my way out of this hole…"

"…Do you know what the first thing Jude ever told me about you was?"

"That we hated each other when we met?"

"No, but he did mention that. He always thought you could do anything you put your mind to. When you decided you were gonna climb that mountain, he doubted you. Then you came back from the top in one piece."

"Barely-"

"And when you left our place for California, the first thing Jude said after you turned out of sight was that now he knew, you really could do anything you put your mind to…"

"I miss him Mary, I miss her, I miss us, I just feel like everything we ever care about, we're just going to lose and I can't-"

"Don't tell me you can't, Mark. You made your bed with Kat, now you've got to sleep in it. Jude is gone and we've got to live with that. This is our life, and there are people here who need us. I know you can do it Mark; just put you mind to it."

On my way out the door to weep and drink that call away, I caught Pops watching a TV special about the moon landing. Magnificent desolation. That's how Buzz Aldrin had described the moon's landscape. Magnificent desolation. I went outside and looked up at the Moon, I just wanted to get away from this world and its seemingly endless griefs.

There was only one tree in our yard. Dark thoughts bloomed from its shadow in the moonlight, thoughts that breed in broken hearts and break the hearts of others. I climbed up through the branches and found a cluster of limbs at the top to support me. There was a moment of peace up there, imagining all the universe swirling around, unconcerned with Earth, or me. I saw the empty darkness of the night and all the little points of light doing their best to brighten it. A faint meteor streaked across the sky. I leaned on the branches and felt myself drifting toward a restful slumber. Then, I felt myself crashing back to Earth.

Dad heard the branches snap, followed by me screaming profanities. He opened the back door to check on me and out came my own little point of light in the darkness, Karma. She rushed over to lick my face and a laugh finally made its way out of my mouth.

"Daddy is broken sweetheart…"

She sat down beside me and put her head on my shoulder.

"You lost a best friend once too, didn't' you Karma. Do remember you learning to let go? Can you to teach me how you got so good at it?"

She licked the leaves and dirt off my face.

"No matter how bad things get, you're always here for me Karma. I love you."

We got up out of the dirt and limped back inside to clean out all the cuts and scrapes I'd gathered on my way down. She sat beside me as I stood there in the mirror. My eyes were swollen and bloodshot, my face was gaunt, my hair unkept, my body looked weak, and I was covered in blood and dirt.

"This is not the character I meant to play…"

Karma tilted her head in confusion.

"I always wanted to be the hero… that thing in the mirror looks more like a monster to me."

She leaned her head back and smiled. In her way, she told me I was her hero.

"It's nobody's fault but mine you know. There are just so many things… and I lost track of what was important."

She stepped closer and rubbed her head against my leg. I'd spent so much time running and hiding from pain, maybe all my life up to then with self-medication and distraction, fruitless pursuits of pleasure that had only ever led to needing more fruitless pursuits of pleasure. I didn't know how, but I felt like it was time to turn and fight.

"I guess this is part where the engine is stripped down to the broken thing and it's time to start putting the pieces back together, isn't it sweetheart?"

Karma stood up with her paws on the counter and leaned her head against my chest, I held her face and she licked my hand.

"I love you too, Karma."

I cleaned myself up and Karma followed me to bed. I lifted her onto the mattress and clutched her in my arms. Then, like a little child and a stuffed animal, we slept.

Karma and I moved out to Peter's cottage for six weeks. In those first few mornings, as soon as I tried to move, I threw up. I would drag myself into the shower and sit there under the hot water until it ran cold, just to feel warmth. I was so cold, always so cold.

The visions that had haunted my dreams became nightmares. My mind tormented my heart, using every memory I had against me. Any hope I tried to hold melted into despair. I would come back to a room in the dark and the shadows would mold themselves into shapes of the lost and the dead. I would hear voices whispering in the breezes moving through the trees. At its worst, reality faded away and the visions were all I could see with my open eyes. Sometimes a dream, sometimes a memory, most often a nightmare.

Then, it started to get better. By the end of our second week, we were spending our days reading and watching the sun roll over the chickens. Karma had outgrown chasing them and was now content to lay there in the grass and watch them eat bugs. In week three, I noticed the chickens didn't seem to envy the birds that flew over their heads. They just went on with their life of taking care of each other, making eggs, and keeping the yard mosquito free for us.

It was around that time, Peter called me to the barn to show me his new tool. It was just a bunch of pipes welded together, with a propane tank hanging off the side and a leaf blower jammed into the back. There was some kind of concrete stuff in the biggest pipe, and it seemed like whatever this was, that was the business end. His eyes were wide when he turned on the gas and struck a match.

"Watch thi-"

Before he finished, the gas hit the match. A giant flaming portal opened ten feet tall in his barn and we both took a huge step back. As flames licked the rafters, Peter let out a sinister cackle.

"It's okay, she just needs air!" he said.

He leaned into the infernal gate and flipped a switch on the leaf blower. The flames flashed out, dimming the daylight, then a sound like a jet-engine and all the fire was swirling blue in the concrete lined pipe on his contraption.

"Is this a forge?" I asked.

"Exactly that! I told Rose I got it fix stuff on the farm, but I'll tell you – I wanna get into knifemaking and metal art."

"Dude, I want your first blade! What got you on this kick?"

"There's been a few times I could've use a forge or a blacksmith… but really, it's the idea that you can throw a common thing into a fire, beat it to death, then grind away everything on the outside, and you end up with something useful and maybe even beautiful."

In week four the rooster found something tasty in the grass and called his hen's over. He saved none for himself as he eyed me like a bum. I couldn't help but agree, I needed a job. I'd never really felt called to one line of work; video games, travel, and partying had always been what I joked were my callings in life. Games were the only thing that could possibly pay, but I'd never learned to write programs or make graphics, so I decided that's what I was going to do. I was going to learn whatever I needed to learn to make a game. But what game?

As the steady ping of Peter's hammer rang like a bell across the farm, I watched Karma wander the field. She looked adventurous with the weeds in the foreground and the trees behind her. My game was going to be about the adventures of a boy and a magic dog. Maybe a blacksmith and a few swords. Maybe even a princess. It was going to be basic old school 1980s graphics, so my focus was going to be finding work that would help me learn programming.

I decided to call Robert up to see if he had any jobs in the area. We caught up first; he confessed to having gone through a similar ordeal to mine after his first divorce.

"It's way easier the second time man!"

"That's comforting… I guess. So… I'm unemployed after

all that. You got any work?"

"Whaddya wanting to do?"

"Development, but I'm nowhere near qualified yet. Anything to get me back in tech and on the road to code works for me."

"When ya looking to start?"

"Two, maybe three weeks at the earliest?"

"A bunch of the young bucks are jumping ship to chase their dreams, as they say, plus we're expanding. There are several support positions opening in a month or so… It's help-desk, but Devs interact with those teams a lot, and its work-from-home. I can maybe get you one of those spots and you can try to move up when some knucklehead abandons his post to wander the earth. If you can you wait that long?"

"That sounds like the perfect maybe. I'll make a resume and send it over. Thanks brother."

"We'll be glad to have you; it's about time your brought your talent back to the table."

Karma enjoyed the freedom of that place, trotting off to meet Peter when she saw him cross the field, sitting by the fence row curiously watching the cows in their pasture, wandering pretty much wherever she pleased without a leash or lead, but never letting herself lose a line of sight on me. Watching her, I started mapping out the world of my game. I made one based on Peter's farm, complete with chickens and blacksmith's forge. I just wanted to pack up some of the peace of that place to take with us, hopefully to share with the world.

Our retreat ended on her 12th birthday. Peter and Rose walked down from their house, Mom and Dad were both there. Everyone looked brighter to me, happier. Karma's parties had always been about her. That one was different. It was about our little flock, doing our best to take care of each other.

Chapter Seventeen

Peter's former boss was looking for help at the shelter. I offered to help while I waited for Robert, on condition that Peter agreed to come and train me for a week. While he was showing me the ropes, a couple of Australian Shepherds came in, two brothers. We were partial to them, being brothers ourselves. One of them took ill, just laying around, struggling to go, and not wanting to eat. We really wanted those brothers to have each other and put extra time into helping that little guy. We would finish our chores, leave for dinner, and come back to check on him. One afternoon, the poor guy could barely move at all. Peter pulled his lips back and looked at his gums; they were white as paper. Peter's shoulders sank with a sigh.

"What?" I asked.

"His gums. It's bad when they get white like that."

He ran up to the cabinet and got a bottle of corn syrup, then came back and rubbed it in his mouth. The little guy perked up some, he even gave us each a few licks.

"Sometimes a little sugar can help, but this little guy is gonna have to fight if he doesn't wanna let his brother down."

The next morning, the little guy was gone, and his brother was left alone in the world. We didn't say much. We dug a grave and, with his brother beside us, stood in silence for a moment before filling it in.

I saw that the shelter wasn't the place for me. The owner found steady help and Mom ended up volunteering out there since her siblings were helping more with Nana. She said she just wanted to stay busy, but I'm pretty sure she just wanted to play with puppies.

One of our favorite games released an anniversary version around that time. The game world was going to be just like it was on day one, before years of expansion changed everything. I brought it up to Peter, nostalgic about those nights we spent trying to learn our characters and work with our teams. He hadn't touched a game in ages, but he eventually agreed to sign up with me. I promised Karma she would always come first, I assumed he did the same with Rose.

The game was the same, but we were different. We were smarter. More patient. And we knew all the tricks and secrets. We burned out on it before the first frost, and I put all my gaming energy back to making my Karma game.

Nana's Thanksgiving was potluck again. The plan was to schedule everyone in small groups to keep Nana from getting over-stimulated. There was going to be a do-over of Christmas at Peter's, but everyone was going to pitch in on the meal and cook it all there together.

Mom called to confirm what time we were coming by Nana's, and she said she had news.

"I'm bringing someone new to Thanksgiving and Christmas."

"Oh, okay… Who?!?"

"Her name is Maggie, she's that little lab puppy from the shelter!"

I wanted to ask if she had any idea what she was getting into with a puppy, but one look at Karma assured me it would all be worth it.

"I can't wait to welcome her to the family!"

When we got to Nana's, she was having a good day. She couldn't get enough of the warm ball of chocolate fur curled up in her lap. Karma went straight for Maggie, and within one sniff, had adopted the pup as her own. She sat with Nana and Maggie the whole time and gazed at them both, wagging her tail anytime Maggie woke up to sniff her new family and making room anytime Nana tried to stand up.

At Christmas, our flock gathered around Peter's table while Maggie chased Karma around it. His fireplace warmed his home, his kitchen warmed our food, and we all warmed each other's hearts.

Then, a single word infected the new year as soon as it began. COVID. It hit home hard for Nana. The regular rhythm of her family in and out of her house had kept her afloat, but she was quarantined well before the word 'lockdown' started circulating in the news. Within days of confirmed cases, her medical team had her, Mom, my uncle, and my aunt all tested and recommended that if they couldn't quarantine with her, they just needed to stay away.

The siblings had all been taking turns keeping Nana. Mom was staying at Peter's cottage on her weeks off. After talking to the medical team, Mom, and her sister, both being retired, sorted out keeping themselves quarantined while still alternating primary care of Nana. My uncle was still working and took on venturing into the stores to stock them up on supplies.

We all called her. Mom used her phone to video chat with us while Nana watched; puzzled and enthralled with the faces and voices of her loved ones talking to her through a sci-fi gadget. It wasn't the same as sharing a room with someone, and Nana felt that. It was a novelty to her at best.

Nana was living in lockdown for over a month before the rest of us learned what that was actually like.

I spent my time at home with Karma and rarely had cause, or money, to go out. The job Robert had gotten me was work-from-home, so it wasn't that much different for me when the lockdown orders came. With her Gramps, as we now called Pops, bored out of his mind and everything on TV reminding him he was trapped at home; Karma became his primary source of sanity. She loved every last second of it.

They spent that whole strange time pacing the house, playing in the living room, and watching DVDs of old TV shows they'd found in the garage. I spent my lockdown walking people through their computer problems over video-chat and piddling with my little game. I really started to admire the bond that had developed between my little girl and my old man. They were the center of each other's world, and it wasn't long before she traded sleeping on my floor to sleeping on his.

Mom dropped by around my birthday to put my present on the porch, we let Karma out to see her, having by now heard that dogs couldn't transmit it. We were the only three people Karma saw until her annual checkup about a week before her own birthday.

It was eerie going out into an empty world on the way to Karma's appointment. All the stores were closed, the streets were empty, and everything was quiet. When I got to the vet, there was a freshly bleached crate outside. They had instructed me to place her in there, then ring the doorbell and go back to my car. Karma looked horrified in that crate, watching me get back in the van. I assured her I was not abandoning her and as soon as the tech came out to get her, she relaxed and followed the young woman inside to see Doc.

I just sat there in the stillness of a world shut down, it was like the peace of Peter's cottage had found its way out into the world and I refrained from thinking about the nightmare that had caused that. I wondered how the world would change if everyone just stopped going to work and started working together to survive. The sound of the tech's voice pierced the ponderous silence after an uncounted collection of minutes.

"Here you go, Doc will call you."

She started to put Karma back in the cage.

"You can just let her go; she'll jump in the car." I shouted.

The tech looked nervous for a moment but scanned the empty highway behind me and noted the absolute certainty on my face. Karma did what she had done best for so long, she trotted right over to my door and let me help her into the van.

The phone rang and, in his ever-calm voice, Doc did what doctors must so often do, he delivered sad news.

"Mark… So, she's got some arthritis setting up in her back and hips and I think I feel some lumps in her upper abdomen."

He paused to let that land.

"Okay, what are you thinking?" I asked.

"There's a few things it could be…"

The only word I understood from the list was cancer.

"If she were a younger dog, we would probably do exploratory surgery, but at her age, I just don't know if it's worth putting her through that, or even if she'd make it through."

Memories of my butchered pup collided with the memories of Grace's last battles in her war with cancer and I locked up for a moment. Doc continued when he heard me breathe.

"…I went ahead and pulled blood to run some tests on, I will call you back when the results are in, and I can answer any questions. I am sorry we had to have this conversation on the phone Mark."

"No, thank you Doc, I'll just… Just, thank you."

She looked fine, bright eyed and smiling, but after just those few words exchanged, she was different to me.

I made up my mind, right in that moment, to lie. To spare my family the fear and helplessness and to carry that burden myself. She was about to be 13, life expectancy of her breed was 12-14 years, they all had enough to worry about, so I decided to keep it from them all, even Karma. I hugged her up close.

"You're a good healthy girl Karma, I love you."

She lit up at my praise, and I smiled back at her. But inside, I can't tell you how hard I cried.

It was her 13th birthday, and it was the first year she didn't get a party. Mom brought over her presents, and she opened them in the yard, me and Dad watched from the door. She paced back and forth from Mom to us, whimpering for us to come join the fun, we just kept saying…

"We can't Karma, COVID, we can't, but we love you!"

Same as we did with Nana through the phone. It was a bittersweet celebration, even more so knowing what I knew.

I spent that night looking through the pictures of our ramblin' days. I dug out our old map and looked at all the states we had been to, and all the ones we hadn't. Somehow, we had missed Arkansas, just a few hours away. I got sad, then mad, then I decided I didn't care about a quarantine, we were checking more states off that map. When we sat down on the couch for our nightly re-run hour. I just told Dad,

"I think I'm gonna take Karma on a ride tomorrow, don't worry if we're not here when you wake up, we'll be back."

Before the sun lit the next morning's clouds, we were on the road. There was nothing in Arkansas I wanted to see, so I decided West Memphis was good enough to check that state off our list. I had folded my back seats down and laid out a thick blanket, then put her favorite bed, Solly's bed, on top of it. Of course, she wasn't having that. She insisted on sitting in her seat, right beside me. We drove off into the sleeping world as we had done so many times before, but this time, even as the sun climbed away from the horizon, the world didn't wake up. We had it all to ourselves.

She sat up through the sunrise, watching the morning pass in a blur of green and blue and grey, but within an hour, it was clear she was getting uncomfortable. She almost fell over every time we hit the slightest bump and by the time we reached the gas station just across the river - our humble destination - I could see that those few hundred miles had taken their toll on her. I pulled out my phone and found a riverside park nearby that allowed dogs. We sat in the grassy field of our private world, not a soul in sight, barely a sound to be heard, and we watched the sun crawl across the sky together.

At dusk I lifted my little girl back into the van for what I knew was going to be her last road trip. Rather than go for the passenger seat, she made her way back to her bed in the back and curled up in it, thirty-two states under her paws, thirty-three counting home. I looked back to check on her after starting up the engine. She raised her head and rolled her bright eyes up to mine. We exchanged smiles and started our journey home.

I had learned not to chase Kat when she ran through my

mind, but passing back through Memphis, with Karma in the back and an empty seat at my side, I found I had little choice. I had heard through Mary that she had graduated, passed the Bar, and was practicing at the same firm that had taken her on as an assistant in the beginning. I was proud of her. It all seemed so far away, like the memory of a dream. I still missed her, the nights of Karma sandwiched between us, but there was a fondness in the longing, and less despair. I was glad for the time we'd shared and hoped that she was too.

As the lights of Memphis passed us by, visions of Katherine passed with them. I adjusted my rearview to show me Karma, sleeping peacefully in her favorite bed. About an hour before home, I saw her stir and with a quick stretch and several stumbling steps, my faithful co-pilot was right there beside me, sitting and smiling, ready to finish our ramblin' the same way it had started… together.

There was no talk of holidays that year, just phone calls and quiet nights. The world was moving again, but with no vaccine, our family was still talking through smartphone screens and storm doors. Nana still called me Sweetpea and always asked about Karma, but she had forgotten so much of the story of our lives. We retold our old tales like they were new, and to her – they were. Nana never changed in her heart, her love for her family never faded, even when the memories of them did. Christmas brought hope, there was news of a vaccine. A chance that we might be able to get back to Nana's house, to our family around a table, to something resembling the way things used to be.

I sat down in front of my computer after talking with Nana on Christmas night. When I pulled up my game and started hacking at code, I realized I hadn't touched the story part of it at all. I started telling myself a story about this boy and this dog who went out to see the world. They wandered forests and climbed mountains; they saw oceans and rode an emerald dragon. They were happy with their travelling life, but at the top of one of those mountains, they looked down and saw the little village they once called home. They wondered what was happening there without them and decided to venture back. That's when they realized they were lost. I stopped to wonder if they would make it back home, or if the game would lead them to some unforeseen destiny, or if maybe the player would choose. Fiction is supposed to be better than reality, so I decided that these two were always going to make it home. That's when things really started to come together. Within a night, I had the whole game planned out and scheduled for release in the spring.

I started taking Karma out to Peter's cottage on Mom's weeks with Nana. It was easier to work out there and Karma could roam the fields. During the weeks Mom was there, we visited and talked, Karma did her best to pass on the years of wisdom she'd gained to Maggie and Mom decided she wanted to start a non-profit after her time at the shelter.

"I wanna pair classrooms with retirement homes. Like to setup kids visiting people in facilities… kinda like mentors for the kids and company for the people in the homes."

"That sound like a great idea, how can I help?"

"Thank you! I'm just now figuring everything out, I'm not even sure where to start."

"You'll figure it out. Work gives us days off to volunteer at non-profits, you can start your foundation with all my volunteer time guaranteed."

Somewhere in the back and forth of that conversation, I remember saying I wished I'd listened to my elders more.

There was a ship stuck in the Suez canal that looked to me like the perfect metaphor for my life, of which I had been captain. My feelings that I'd piloted my ship into the banks and that I should have listened to my elders more were never more true than the morning I woke up 40 years old.

Karma's 14th birthday fell on a week Mom was at Nana's. I had finished my game and set it for release the morning of Karma's birthday. It seemed right to release it on that day; If me and Peter were the only two that played it, there would still be cause for celebration.

Unfortunately, it was not one of Nana's better days. Somehow, she remembered Karma's life better than she remembered her own. I made a meal, drawing on all the cooking show marathons and line-cook skills of days gone by. For Karma, I made a little unseasoned meatloaf 'cake' with mashed potato 'frosting', then used her kibble to write out a '14' on the top. Mom had wrapped up a couple of small presents for Maggie to open, hoping Karma could teach Maggie the art. Karma got treats, chew toys, and a padded harness with a handle so I could help my her up the steps without risking my own back in the process. Maggie looked on in bewilderment.

I had made a caramel pie for dessert and, as we were all sipping coffee and nibbling at that, I told Nana I'd finished my video game and released it that morning.

"Good for you Sweetpea! Good for you!! That meal sure was wonderful, did Katherine make all that for us? When is she comin'???" she asked.

It had happened before. Once, I'd told her we weren't together anymore and the grief in her face forced me to lie every time since. There are lots of times in life when the truth just doesn't matter.

"Kat had to work Nana, she's in court helping people. She's a lawyer now!"

"Oh, I'm so proud of her! An' so glad you two are together!"

"She sends her love Nana; she loves you like her own grandma!"

"I bet she's ashamed to wear that little ring of mine ain't she!"

"Not at all Nana! She wears it every day and is prouder of that one than she'd be of any ring I ever could've bought!"

It was painful to lie, but unbearable to tell the truth. The smile it brought to Nana's face was all the reassurance Mom and I needed to know Nana deserved something better than the truth.

"She is the sweetest thing, and so pretty too – you picked a good one Sweetpea, and Karma, you're sweet and pretty too!"

As she leaned over to feed Karma a piece of her caramel pie, I noticed Nana's hair was as white as Karma's. I didn't have the heart to stop them, they'd both earned their treats.

"I know Nana, I'm a lucky man!"

Chapter Eighteen

Nana got worse after that. She kept saying, "I just wish I could get better so I could live my life. I just want to go home!"

But she was at home. All we could tell her was that we loved her, and we were there to help.

On her last visit before the holidays, the hospice nurse had told us it would be a few weeks before we had to say goodbye. The word was spread, but no plans were made. Nana couldn't get out of bed, we couldn't have Thanksgiving, we were just waiting. When we visited, we were just watching, and in the bitter cold of that winter, we were just hoping – one more Thanksgiving, one more Christmas, one more New Year.

Dad's phone rang in the afternoon on Thanksgiving Day.

"Hello?"

Silence.

"We'll be over there in a minute."

He didn't have to say anything when he came to my room, I already had all my things together, I had already told Karma I would be back later and promised her I'd take Nana her love.

"I know Pop, let's go."

I just kept telling myself, all the struggle Nana was going through, it was all about to be over for her and she could rest. She was going to be free from the prison her body had become. I told myself so many things I'd never believed in those few miles; that she was going to see Grandpap, that she was going to play with Grace, that she was going to rejoice and be happy in a heaven up above, in a place where all her family could be around her table and only talk about how blessed they were to have each other.

Mom and her siblings were there, gathered around Nana as she slept with labored breath. Then a cousin arrived. Then another. And another with kids. And another, and another. Hours passed without a word said. As the lingering glow of the Sun's light faded from the windows, the last cousin arrived. Ben, from hours away, walked in the door with tears in his eyes.

With every soul she and Grandpap had brought into this world around her, our Nana took her last breath.

Mom reached for her mother's hand.

"We love you Mama… tell Daddy we love him… we love you both…"

All the differences, all the fights, all the things that had quietly pushed our family apart. None of it mattered right then, all that mattered was the blood and the grief we shared.

Katherine was at the funeral. Her grief was no less than any of ours. During the final viewing, on her way back to her pew, she touched my hand as she passed. I felt it give me strength, to help hold up the weight of that metal box our Nana would now sleep forever inside.

I had been through it so many times as a kid with Dad's family that it was an auto pilot. You wait for your cue, you stand up, the director turns the casket, you take your place. You lift. You load it in the hearse, the mourners all move toward their cars, the family all cries, the staff secures the casket, then the pallbearers make the short walk to their vehicles and follow the hearse.

Down south, all the cars in a funeral line turn their lights on. It was the old way, so that all the cars on the road could pull over to let the procession pass. We had a short ride to the cemetery, but it was a busy day. Nana and Grandpap had lived their whole lives in that town – people knew who was in the hearse, and a lot of traffic stopped. The faces I saw mirrored our own grief, even though most were strangers to me.

We had Nana next to Grandpap before I felt what we were doing, what was really happening, what this all really meant. I had seen my Nana for the last time.

We pulled the flowers off our jackets and placed them on her casket, just like we'd done years before, for the man who loved her, and us, unconditionally. The funeral director carried all her flowers to the grave. And everyone took their seats.

I felt bad for Katherine. She was sitting in the back, all alone with strangers, not with Nana's family where she belonged. I sat down beside her and she just leaned on me and cried.

The Reverend finished telling us about Lazarus, we all walked past the casket and paid our final respects. Katherine and I held each other up on our way to the hole Nana's box was held over and she kissed her goodbye. She clutched my arm and I squeezed her hand as we walked back to our seats. The church choir sang. The staff lowered Nana down to her spot next to Grandpap. We all wept, then took the first few steps back to our lives. I walked Katherine to her car.

"I'm glad you came… I know Nana would be too."

"I loved her Mark… I loved her so much."

"She loved you Kat, just like one of her own, just like one of us."

We hugged and felt our tears on each other's cheeks. Then, we said goodbye.

Karma was there for anyone who needed of cheering up. She just wanted everyone to feel better. She and Nana had that in common. Seeing her brighten the family's spirits brightened my own more than anything in those early weeks after Nana's passing. We all huddled around Karma in Mom's living room and she created a magic bubble where it was okay to set down our grief and laugh, where it was okay to be okay. I wanted to be there for my family and Karma let me feel like I was doing that. A magic dog that followed me everywhere I went, to brighten the darkest hours.

Our game slowly gained steam and by the new year I saw my first rent-paying check. The sales supplied a nice windfall but more importantly, opened a window of opportunity. I got an email from a midsize studio looking for new talent. They had played my game and wanted to add me to their team.

Within a handful of messages, and one very awkward video conference that Karma insisted on being a part of, I found myself staring at a job offer for a dream job, paying double the most I'd ever made before. It didn't seem real, sitting there with Karma snoring at my feet, looking at the paycheck they were offering for something I was willing to do for free; and I was going to keep working from home with Karma.

My whole erratic life had brought me to that 5-paragraph email, every failed plan and forlorn hope, every surprise victory and lucky break. I whispered a quiet thank you in my heart to anyone that could hear it and with a few clicks of the mouse, I signed on the dotted line.

When my job began, we found it more like play than work. We made new friends, even some from places we had been. Five days a week my assistant, Karma, was in the office.

Dividing her time between brightening the faces of my co-workers and sleeping on the clock. When the whistle blew, it was a zero-minute commute to the life I had come to cherish, a simple life with simple needs. I wasn't rich, but as my bank account grew, another dream took root. I wanted a home of my own. Not a rented space, not the charity of family or friends, but a piece of land with a house and a deed signed to me, a place for a good life to grow.

Nana's estate was closing around that same time. Mom hated the thought of selling the old place and was rolling through ideas for renting it out or finding someone Nana knew to buy it – I almost choked on my words when I asked.

"What about me?"

"…Is that something you'd want, I mean something you'd want for yourself?"

"Mom, there's no stack of bricks and wood on this earth I'd rather call my home."

"The market is so high right now, are you sure you want to buy in, they all keep saying it's gonna come down soon, maybe we could hold it-"

"No. The memories in that house – happy and sad – are worth more to me than anyone, in any market, would ever pay. Buying that house would not be an investment for me, that's my forever home. Nana and Grandpap left that for you guys, so that you'd have some share of all their hard work through the years, so they could do one last thing to take care of their kids – I wanna help them do that and I will pay whatever price the market demands."

"If it's really what you want, I know we would all love for you to have it!"

"I'll start talking to banks tomorrow, you guys find a fair price and we'll all meet up to talk about making it happen."

She almost crushed my ribs with her hug and then reached down to Karma with joyful tears in her eyes.

"Karmie, do you wanna move to your Nana's house?!"

Karma looked up and licked her Grammie, eyes alight, and smiled.

I had a down payment and income, but all the years of financial turmoil had left me with poor credit. The rest of that month was calls and numbers, rates, and payments; in many cases, just a flat-out 'no' from the lenders. I barely pre-qualified for the loan I got, and it was costly, but it was the loan I deserved and I was thrilled to get it.

Nana's kids gathered around my mother's table and a deal was struck. There was still the matter of all Nanas things though, the things the family hadn't taken. There was also the mountain of leftovers from my shop that waited to topple out onto me every time I opened the garage. We decided that Dad would rescue us, and reclaim his garage, with an auction in the spring.

We rented a 26-foot box-truck and set out to empty Dad's garage in a single weekend. Box after box we loaded until the truck was full, then box after box we unloaded. Then again, and again, until we loaded the last box onto the truck and the only thing of mine left in Dad's garage was the lonely old Rodeo, shimmering emerald green in the sunlight it hadn't seen for years.

I felt cool winds from distant roads make their way across my face. Karma did too. She ran right up to it, sniffing and wagging her tail. Although she was too stiff to jump, she raised her paw to the floorboard when I opened that door we had kept shut for so long. I hoisted her up into the seat and she plopped down into the worn foam hole she had made after all those miles together. I took the driver's seat, and we sat there in the garage for a moment, all the hills and curves and mountains and seas, all the people and places, all passed us by like shooting stars in our minds.

"Who were we Karma?"

The memory had become distant and faint – the adventure made insignificant by the roads we had travelled since. Her puppy hairs still littered everything, grains of sand still glinted in the carpet, our trusty atlas still lay in the pocket of the door, and now, here too were we – back where we once belonged, our own tiny world bound by steel and mounted on wheels.

I looked over at my faithful companion, her hair as white still as the day she was born, and I realized just how long it had been, just how far we had come together for no other reason than because we stayed together. Looking at her over in her seat, eyes fixed out the front glass at an open garage door, I couldn't help but ask.

"Do you wanna go on another adventure Karma?"

She drew back her head and tilted it to the side, then looked out toward the corner of the garage where Mom and Dad were looking on. With a confident step across the console toward the door, she crawled across my lap and pawed the door handle for me to let her out. I opened the door and helped her to the ground. She wasted no time making a clockwork trot to her grandparents, dropping her tail to the ground at their feet, and cutting her brown eyes back to me in an almost defiant stare.

"Me too karma, I wanna stay home too."

I shut the door on that emerald dream and made my way to the half-loaded truck that would bear the last of my hoard to Nana's garage.

"You guys go on over, I'll be there in a few."

"We can get this stuff if you wanna rest, you have to work

in the morning."

"What I do is nothing remotely approaching work, I just wanna sweep up so we don't have to do it later."

We waved and they left, then I grabbed my phone from the van and called my brother's old tow truck friend. My dad's garage was finally going to be all his own again.

Winter melted away the mess of boxes and they became orderly lots. Dad and Peter had lined everything up under a tent, and the warm March sun fought with the cool north winds like the bittersweet mixture of feelings in our hearts as the auction got underway. We had all pulled the items that meant the most to us long before this day came, but a curious thing happened to me. Just two items into the sale, a little black rocking chair was held up in the air, its painted flowers weathered by the backs of countless kids Nana had kept. All those years of memories leapt at me when the sun hit that faded paint. Dad started chanting and I hear someone yell:

"Yeah!!!"

I'd shouted out, without a thought, not even realizing I had bid until my brother's eyes met my own.

That's the trick of an auction, you don't know what you really want until you see someone else might get it. Someone in the front row challenged my bid. We went back and forth until she finally stood to see the determination in my face and gave up hope. An item or two passed and it hit me again, another fragment of a memory cast my bid.

On and on and on it went, they held something up and a memory of Nana would leap off it, and my hand went up. Even as they were selling my stuff, I found memories of conversations with customers at the shop, or something funny Karma had done near the item, and I was buying my own product back at auction. My purchases accounted for half Nana's sales, and I had bought back a quarter of my own junk. Peter was baffled.

"What got into you, you could have kept all that for free!?"

"Just got sucked up in the moment brother, auction fever."

I tried to laugh, but I shocked myself with my behavior. Mom came over after they had gathered all the money and said I didn't have to pay for Nana's things. I insisted – I told her Nana's spirit got into me; to make sure her kids got every dime they could out of her things.

I walked the house after the sale. I wanted to keep it the same, but the old place needed fixing up. I set out to replace the carpet and polish the old hardwoods, wire the place up with a network, get a new roof and update the bathrooms. A new kitchen was also in order but the dining room, I wanted to leave that exactly the same, like museum quality preservation. The outdated paneling and scuffed hardwood was perfect. I'd ended up with Nana's table at the sale, and it was going to sit exactly where it always had, in front of the big window with Grandpap's chair looking out over the back yard.

On Karma's birthday, I called Mom up to ask if she could follow me somewhere,

"Sure, why, is everything okay?"

"Everything is fine, I'm just gonna sell my van and get something else."

"Mark are you sure, you-"

"Already been sold Mom, we're just delivering – we might do a little shopping while were out."

"...Okay."

She followed me out to the dealership I'd sold the van to. In about 15 minutes, my minivan was on its journey to a new, more exciting life, and I had twice what I'd paid for it in hand.

"Do you want to tour some lots?" mom asked.

"Let's check out this junkyard closer to home, he's got some older models cheap I'm told."

I directed her off the beaten path onto a gravel drive. I could feel her tension filling the car.

"I'm gonna see if he's in, you wanna wait here?"

"Okay…" she said, utterly confused.

I saw her face when I drove out from behind the building in a fully overhauled and freshly painted Rodeo. She leapt out of her car to meet me and passed a hug through the window.

"Is this yours?! I mean the one you kept so long? I thought you scrapped it!"

"I sent it here for overhaul, took them forever to find parts."

"It looks brand new!"

"Only on the outside."

I called her attention to Karma's fur in the seat, the sand in the carpets, and all my many coffee stains.

"Awwwww!"

"Follow me home and let's show our birthday girl what daddy got her this year."

We had Karma's 15th birthday party at Nana's old house, now officially my new house. Contractors were still working on the place, but we had them take the day off. Mom set up the party in the back yard, Dad went over early to lend a hand. Peter and Rose made time in their schedules to attend, and I invited Maggie. Me and Karma arrived in a Rodeo reborn, to cheers and a Happy Birthday song. Maggie charged over to the birthday girl and Karma indulged her in as much rough housing as her old bones would let her. Then we turned Peter loose on the grill and the rest of us took turns chatting and playing with the pups.

The hour for presents came and Karma wasted no time getting to her favorite part of the party. One by one the bags and boxes fell to her ferocious fangs, she overlooked the contents until she was sure every scrap of paper and cardboard had been torn down, then she was on to finding the treats among her gifts. Maggie had worn herself out running in the fields but woke up and did her best to take part. She was far more interested in the toys than opening packages, but Karma was so focused on entertaining us that she was none the wiser to her sister's thieving.

The pups played tug with a monkey made of rope, the folks watched and laughed, Peter and Rose cuddled in the swing. The weather was warm and the scene was new, in a familiar old way. The sun went down, Peter and Rose made their way home, and me and the folks sat and talked while Karma paced between us with her rope monkey. That whole party, I don't think she sat down once.

Karma and I wandered the yard a bit after everyone had gone. I thought back to those first few visits to this exact spot and how Nana had told me dogs can teach us about life and love. I wanted to stay that night, but things inside were a mess from the contractors and I had to work. I gave the house a quick once over and checked all the lights and locks before loading Karma into her carriage. We fired that rebuilt engine up and took a quick last look over the backyard before we headed home.

"One more memory planted in that field, Karma."

We weren't home five minutes before Karma drug her bed to Dad's side at the couch, then curled up with her arm around her rope monkey and fell soundly to sleep.

Chapter Nineteen

It was a lazy summer. We made trips to see Maggie and trips to check the house, but mostly we sat on Dad's back porch, watching the wildlife that found its way into his yard. Karma's struggles to get up were becoming clearer. As the days grew shorter, her energy was shortening with them. She was late to work more often, she mostly slept on the clock, and she wasn't as quick to the food bowl at lunch.

Dad was aging himself and sympathized with her – always assuring her, he knew how it was. She stayed quick to make her way to the Rodeo for our rides and she was right there to greet family when they visited, bright eyed as a months old puppy.

We made a trip out to see Nana's grave not long before the contactors finished the house. The wind and the rain had begun to settle her earthen blanket. Karma sat by their stones while I talked to my grandparents.

"I'm moving into your old house Nana; I hope you and Grandpap are happy in your new one. I love you both so much."

Work on the house finished in September and I took what time I had to go over and clean the place up in those first weeks of Fall. I recruited Peter to help me move some things from the garage into the house, most challengingly, Nana's oak dining table. We pulled some leaves to make a six-seater and lined it up with the window like Nana had kept it. I promised him a no hassle Thanksgiving meal for his trouble.

By the time we sat down, it was almost exactly like Nana's dining room, right down to the brown drip-ware dishes I'd never paid attention to until they were on the auction block. The kitchen had gotten a thorough upgrade, but at the end of that day, you could feel it. It was Nana's place. Peter called attention to it first.

"It's like we're just kids hangin' out at Nana's again, brother."

"Thanks for your help, man, I'm happy with the way it's turned out."

"So… Thanksgiving at your place this year, Christmas at mine? You need any help?"

"I do actually have a list of stuff I could use off the farm, food prices are insane with this global shortage going on. Also, I could probably use Rose for backup in the kitchen."

"Take anything you need, and I'm sure she'd be glad to help. I better be gettin' on back to her – if I don't see you before, I'll see ya then."

It almost felt like home. Except Karma was missing. With that thought I switched off all the lights, locked the doors, and made my way back down the road to her and her Gramps.

I requested a week off to move but we were so busy, I had to settle for just a Thursday and a Friday. The weeks flew by under the crush of trying to finish our projects before the holiday break. I trickled things over to the house, did some arranging and rearranging, but really didn't get a lot done. On Wednesday of moving week, they let me clock out after our lunch huddle – everyone wished me and Karma well and said they were excited to see our new home. I pulled her up into my lap to wave bye to everyone and we clocked out for the week.

I felt compelled to jump right into packing, but I opted to kick back with Karma and stream a movie. She raised her paw up on the bed saying she would like to join me. I helped her up and she laid out beside me with her head on my chest. We took turns watching TV and taking naps until well past working time that next morning. I couldn't remember the last time she had spent the whole night on the bed with me, having preferred her own bed and if possible, her Gramps floor, for a long time now. I had forgotten how nice it was to have her warmth there. I also realized my princess was well overdue a bath and added it to my to-do list.

Thursday was all packing and preparation; I had done zero disassembly of our living arrangements and somehow, in one day, I dismantled years of accumulated life and gathered it all neatly into boxes. When I got to Karma's bath on my to-do list, I hoisted her over into the tub and got the water running. She struggled to keep her feet and looked at me with pitiful eyes, I just climbed into the tub and supported her while I washed her up. I gave her a hug and she lapped a drop of water off my face. As I helped her out of the tub, I just about busted my own tail trying to stand up in wet jeans on my ageing knees. After a quick shake and good towel drying, she slept in the living room while I thought about all the work we had to do in the next few days.

It was non-stop for two days. Dad and Peter were helping me with their trucks, Mom was watching Maggie and Karma, and Rose brought us lunch and dinner. I was worried that moving my things into Nana's house would obscure the memories I wanted to preserve, but with each thing I unpacked, it was like those memories shined through even brighter, like we were just adding to the story of that old place. By Saturday night everything was out of Dad's house except my little girl and her bed.

Karma was pacing through the house when I got back. I helped her down the stoop and left the door open for her to come back inside when she finished. I paced through the house myself to make sure I hadn't missed anything and looked back at all the memories we had made in that house, even memories of my great grandparents when they lived there bubbled to the surface. It was so full of them now and so strange to be leaving them. When I was sure that memories were the only things I was leaving behind, I noticed Karma wasn't back in yet.

I checked out back and she had fallen. She was sitting there like Grace used to in the early days of her hips failing. I told her it would be all right and leaned over to help her up; she gave a little lick as I got close. With her hips in hand, I helped her up and she let out a faint whimper.

"I'm sorry sweetheart, too fast?"

I helped her take those first few steps to the door, then went to wait for her at the stoop. When I got there and looked back, she was standing still, head down, right where I had left her.

"It's okay Karma, you can come on in…"

She tried to take a step and stopped. I went back to help her, but she didn't want to move. We slowly inched toward the door with me spotting her, step by step. She never made a sound but just didn't want to move. I thought about when I messed my back up and worried that she had pulled something. We took our time going inside and over to her bed in the living room. She laid down and let out a long sigh.

I left her there to shut the back door and she tried to get up but whimpered and laid back down. I remembered so clearly going through that transition with Grace and I sat there a minute, adjusting myself to the idea that this was going to be more of our days together until they ran out. A ride in this condition seemed inconsiderate and usually Grace was better after a night's sleep.

"It's okay if you don't want to leave yet sweetheart, we can stay here another night."

I kissed her on the head and went back to my room with a blanket, thinking we would just camp there and move to our new home in the morning.

When I was out of sight, she made a long whistling whine, like I was leaving her behind. I went back in to soothe her and something in the way she was laying, that play-dead pose we never practiced again after surgery. I flipped on the overhead light and could see something was wrong.

When I knelt to check her, I noticed her usually pink skin was paler. I checked her gums, and they were white. It felt like all the blood in my own body fell out.

I woke Dad up and told him something was wrong with Karma. Doc was getting ready to retire and had stopped doing emergency services so I called Mom for her vet's number, she said she would find it and call them. I called Peter and after telling him what I was seeing, he said he was on his way. Dad and I were beside her on the living room floor, she was trying so hard to get up and engage with us but couldn't seem even sit-up. We tried to calm her, and ourselves. Our fears were fanning into panic by the time Mom arrived. Karma leaned her head up and tried to get to her Grammie, Mom rushed over to her and got right down in Karma's face so she wouldn't have to move.

Mom noticed her gums immediately and said she had called the emergency vet in the next town and was waiting for a call back. A moment of silence passed; a sense of anguish began filling the room. We were all crying when Peter arrived. Before he could even evaluate the situation, Mom's phone rang. I answered and explained to the Vet what was happening, she was kind and gentle – she said it did not sound good, especially for a pup Karma's age. I was trying to get my head around everything that was happening, and Mom's trembling voice cracked.

"Please… let's just take her… can we please take her?"

I told the Vet we were on our way, and she instructed me where to park. Peter and I made eye contact and with nothing else said, grabbed the ends of her bed and carried Karma to Mom's car. We sat her across the back and even in that weakened condition she looked happy to be going on a ride, especially one with Grammie at the wheel. I got in the passenger seat, for lack of room in back, and reached back to rest my hand on Karma's heart. She had her head up trying to look around and I told her we were going to get her some help. She looked over at her Grammie, who gave her a tearful smile and Karma laid her head down on the seat.

I just kept my hand and my eyes on Karma and Mom negotiated the 10-minute drive to the Vet. Peter and Dad went in Peter's truck, they were not far behind when we arrived. Mom transferred her attention to Karma once we parked and I ran to the door to ring the bell. A young woman in scrubs answered with a solemn tenderness in her voice,

"You can bring her in here." She said.

"Thank you"

I got back to the car as Peter and Dad pulled in, Peter was out of his truck before his engine fully stopped and we had

Karma on her way to the table.

It was worse, she was so pale, so weak looking, like she couldn't hold her mouth closed or her tongue in it. Still, she acknowledged the Vet and gave her a half-smile when she introduced herself. We all crammed into the room around the stainless-steel table and as soon as the Vet felt her abdomen, her shoulders sank and her eyes dulled. She did her best to tell me gently and professionally that it felt like there was 'free fluid' in Karma's abdomen – meaning blood. Then, she grabbed an ultrasound machine to confirm. She looked at the screen and tender announced,

"It looks like a tumor on her spleen has ruptured."

I knew. I told her I understood. I knew what that meant. I knew it was time.

My whole life with the little girl on that table played out in memory, it felt like every second, like every feeling, like our whole story ran from reel to reel. To everyone else in the world, it was a fraction of a second, but to four of the people in that room it was almost 16 years of joy and sadness… of struggle and victory… and of love… unconditional love every day.

Mom, Dad, Peter, and Karma – I just took turns looking at them all, being so grateful they were there, so glad for Karma, for all of us that if this was the end, that her whole family was around her. She never showed it, but I know she was hurting.

"Let's take this pain for her." I said.

The Vet cast a heartbroken look my way and left to get the injections. We all caved in around her, around our Karma, our little girl. We sobbed as quietly as we could, we all tried to show Karma how much she had meant, how special she was, how lucky we felt to have her. We all took turns at her face;

she'd grown too weak to lift her head.

I was the last and was holding her face when the Vet came back in. Karma was so tired, so sleepy looking. The Vet tried to set up a line in her back leg but there was no blood flow. She moved to the front and Mom held the paw she was working with while Peter held Mom and kept a hand on Karma. Dad was at Karma's back rubbing her with both hands. I knelt down in her face and looked into her beautiful brown eyes and dried my tears.

"It's okay to let go sweetheart, you've been the best Karma and I love you… don't be afraid… it's okay to let go. I promise we'll be okay, and I will look after your Grammie and your Gramps for you…"

It was so hard to breathe, I choked back another wave of tears and kissed her.

"…I'm so glad you picked me. I feel so special to have been your daddy Karma."

I closed my eyes and kissed her again on her nose. She moved her tongue to my face, and I rubbed her ears as she gave me our last kiss.

She drew a deep breath, and my little girl closed her eyes as her last breath gently eased out of her.

The room was silent. The Vet hadn't given her anything yet. We all knew she was gone, we all felt the moment she left our lives. I nodded for the Vet to continue and after she had injected everything, she checked for a pulse. She looked at me and expressed a bittersweet smile that said Karma was resting. When she quietly left the room, I collapsed on the door frame. Peter gave both his shoulders to the folks, each with a hand on their granddog. There were no words. She was my child, my sister, my friend, and my family; and she was gone.

Mom and I composed ourselves enough to see the Vet. We decided to have Karma cremated. Mom helped me through everything, and the Vet assured me they would cremate Karma by herself and would take a paw print for us. We got the arrangements made and it wasn't until we got back to the room that I realized Karma wasn't coming home. I realized that it was the last time I would ever see her, feel her fur on my fingertips, hold her paw in my hand, or rub her velvet ears, or kiss her cold nose.

We told Peter and Dad we were cremating her, that this was it. It was 2 am. It was just the four of us and a gentle stranger, and it was time to say goodbye to Karma. We each took our turn soaking her fur with tears, Gramps who she had watched over so well, her Grammie who had thrown her parties and loved her like a child, her Uncle Peter, who she had started life with and who'd helped to mold her into who she became, and then me… The luckiest of all, her daddy.

It killed me to leave her. When the door clicked behind me, I heard someone wail, and I just walked. I felt that it was me wailing, and I just walked. I was all the way to the road before I could breathe, it felt like memory was all that was left of me.

The streets were empty, the lights flashing red and yellow, the faint sounds of HVAC units in the stillness of the night. I was taken back to quiet nights on the road with Karma, where the only sounds to be heard were her snores and the humming of the Rodeo carrying us through the dark. Karma always kept an open heart; she always took everything in stride. I thought about that, there in the pale orange streetlight glow. I turned back toward my family. I was in their arms before I knew it and under the streetlamps and the stars, we grieved together.

Mom and I took her car home, she crumpled in the

passenger seat and held my hand while I tried to see through the wall of water perched on my eyelashes.

"She was so good…"

"She was the best, Mom. She was the best…"

Turning the ignition off was the last bit of focus I had before the sorrow overtook me again. I folded my arms on the steering wheel and laid my head on them to weep until Peter and Dad got there.

The four of us made our way inside to the silence – a house once filled with the tiny noises of cats and dogs, a mother, a father, and their children, now only held the hollow sound of four broken hearts beating. We sat. We stared at her bed she'd stolen from Solly, at her fur on everything around us, at the uneaten food in her bowl, the undrunk water. An unopened bag of dog food leaned in the corner, useless. We sat sad but grateful to be un-alone in that grief.

Nothing could be said, nothing needed to be said. We all felt the same and words would only get in the way of communication. We drank stale coffee until the sun came up, then we greeted a bittersweet dawn. The conversations we had that night were of the purest language, they were Karma's language, spoken with our eyes and our expressions, our postures, our hugs, and our tears. The sun lit the world again and we said quiet goodbyes. Peter and Mom went home, Dad made his way to bed, and I went to my empty room.

Chapter Twenty

I laid there on the carpet of that empty room, in that house where Karma and I had lived half her life. It smelled like her. Whisps of fur clung to my black hoodie and every time I moved, I picked up what seemed like a hundred more. A lone flea jumped on my face wondering where his host had gone. I was out of tears, I couldn't sleep, I couldn't get up. I just started going through all of our pictures, over a thousand moments of our life together, frozen in time. Scenes from our first house, from the road. From our full house days, from the days at the apartment with Katherine. Moments at Nana's and Peter's farm, moments I'd completely forgotten.

The sun crept through the blinds as it burned away the clouds and brought memories of all the people Karma had met in her life, all the lives she had touched. I got online and started scrolling my friends. I saw the old neighborhood kids all grown up, with dogs and children of their own. It reminded me just how long Karma and I had been together, how much time I'd really had with her. It seemed like it all passed in the stroke of a second hand. I just felt like they all should know, or maybe I just didn't want to grieve her alone, I don't know but I made a post. It was my first in years. I used a picture of Karma in my passenger seat, looking out over the ocean as we drove down the Pacific Coast Highway, and wrote.

"Last night this angel in dog's fur earned her wings. Thank

you to everyone who loved her with me."

I felt so fortunate to have been a part of it all, so grateful for her, so grateful for everything in that moment and I finally slept.

My phone was filled with condolences when I woke up. One from Katherine read,

I am so sorry you lost Karma, my thoughts are with you and your family.

There was a broken heart after the words. It wasn't much, but it brought her into the room with me and warmed the air.

Thank you, I know you loved her too

I wrapped myself in the blanket I had gathered for us to sleep on the night before and made my way to the living room where Dad was listless on the couch. We were silent, we couldn't look at each other, just down at Karma's empty bed in the corner. Mom arrived not long after and together we sat with our memories of the joys we had shared with Karma and with the grief we now shared without her. Mom finally broke the silence.

"I just can't believe she's gone…"

Then, we all took that first step toward healing. We started talking. We recounted the good times, shared our shock, expressed the emptiness we all felt sitting in that room without her. The sunset painted the room a brilliant orange, and I made my way back to my phone. Katherine had sent a message.

I'd like to see you sometime, when you're feeling up to it?

Is tonight too soon?

Not at all, just tell me when and where.

Give me an hour. Same old place?

I'll meet you there.

She was waiting when I arrived, sitting at one of the now shoddy tables that had scuffed the color off the tile floor through the years. She stood to greet me and gave me a hug.

"Thank you for meeting me." I said.

"I'm so sorry for your loss, Mark."

"Thank you. Have you ordered?"

"Not yet"

"Let's get you caffeinated; I could use your chattiness."

We made our way to the counter and ordered our usuals then sat back at our table.

"If you don't want to talk about it, I understand… but what happened?"

"It was a tumor on her spleen, it ruptured."

"She was such a good girl… How is your family taking it?"

"We were all there, around her on the table, I was glad of that for Karma, and for us. We're sticking together. We got over fifteen good years with her… We're grateful."

"I just can't believe she's gone…"

"I know… She was slowing down, but I never expected she was about to stop, especially the day she was going to her forever-"

The word 'home' stuck in my throat… Karma had gone to her forever home.

"I heard you bought Nana's house... Congratulations. I confess to being nosy about that."

"What do you mean?"

"I had our real estate team watching for it to go on the market. I wanted to tour it before it sold. I have so many good memories there and I... well, I think about your Nana a lot. I wanted to walk through it again... to see it one last time... and maybe feel close to her again before-"

The server brought our cups, he had made little hearts in the froth that brought a breath of amusement into the somber air around our table.

"Tell me about your practice?" I asked.

"It's busy... Sometimes, I wonder if what I'm doing is really helping anybody."

"I'm sure it is. Pops felt like that a lot when he was in Family Law, but he looks back on it now and can see the good he did."

"I hope so..."

"Nana used to say that sometimes it's hard to see the good you're doing for someone in tough times because the times are tough." I laughed at the memory "She also said tough times make tough people."

"Your Nana was really smart about people; I can't tell you how many times I'll be listening to a client and something Nana said will pop into my head."

"She was a wise one... I guess all those years on earth teach you a few things. We talked a lot while she was here... I wish I'd listened more."

"I am really glad her house stayed in the family; she would have loved that."

I could feel the tears trying to well up with all the memories of Nana and Karma stirring to the surface.

"It's pretty close to how Nana left it. If you want to see it again, we can get these coffee's to-go. I know she'd like that. Plus… I feel like if we sit here much longer, all these people are gonna see me cry."

She searched my eyes, I could see her own tears welling up.

"I'd like that." she said softly.

We walked to the counter for to-go cups and out into the mostly empty lot.

"Oh my god, is that THE Rodeo!"

"Indeed, it is. Called back from its tomb."

"It looks just like it did the first time you picked me up in it!"

"Only on the outside. So, you know the way - I'll meet you there?"

With a nod and a smile in response, she followed me home.

We got to the door and I opened it for her.

"I'll give you some time. Make yourself at home, I'm gonna pace the field I think."

"I'd rather you stayed. …you help me remember."

She loved the new kitchen and the dining room was full of Nana's old things. She looked over it all like pieces in a museum and I told her stories I knew. I had a little treasure chest with all Grandpap's silver coins and some of Nana's jewelry displayed in their old dish cabinet. Her ring was sitting right on top.

"Is that Nana's engagement ring? I never saw her wear it."

"Yeah. She said she just couldn't wear it after she met Arthur."

"Arthur?! Who is that?"

"Arthur-itis"

"Stop it right now mister!"

She threw me a playful swat before turning her gaze back to Nana's ring.

"...It's gorgeous."

We talked about Nana, Karma, and Jude. We talked about Us. We talked about life. We came to a silence and she looked almost embarrassed.

"What is it?"

"I don't know if this is the right time for this, but I feel like I need to share it."

She took her phone out of her purse and swiped her finger around a few times.

"This is my puppy. I picked him last week."

She showed me a picture of a dark brindle Frenchie with adorably huge mouse ears.

"He's a lucky man!"

"It will be a few weeks before I can pick him up, I guess I just wanted to show you because I don't know if I ever would've gotten a dog if I hadn't met Karma. Have you thought about what's next for you?"

"I'm not sure. I want to help Mom with her non-profit and work is wanting to send me on the publicity team for the new game, it looks like most of next year will be back and forth to tradeshows. I guess I'm just going to see what maybes I find out there."

When she took her phone back, she noticed the time.

"It's getting late... You must be exhausted Mark."

She looked tired too.

"It is late, if you don't want to drive home, you're more than welcome to stay. The guest bed is brand new."

"Thank you, but I should go."

I helped her gather her things and walked her to her car.

We hugged at her car door. Our hands lingered on each other's arms as we let each other go.

"...It doesn't feel right for us to be strangers, Kat. I don't know where we fit into each other's lives now, or if we even do, but I'd like to see you again sometime."

"I'd like that, thank you for having me. Maybe you can meet my puppy over the Holidays."

"Maybe. Thank you for the visit... Thank you for everything."

With another hug, she closed the door and waved, then started to drive away. I waved until she turned onto the road and drove out of sight.

Back at Dad's place, Peter was sitting up with the folks. Disease and death were weekly visitors to his farm. It hurt Peter, but he saw the cycle, the story playing out for all living things. He knew there was nothing we could have done. Peter's words were wise and gentle and one-by-one he swam us each to shore in that sea of grief. Exhaustion took us, first Mom, then Dad, then me. Peter kept watch on his flock until the last one found their way to bed, then he made his way home.

Monday morning came and I found the folks in the backyard sitting by Grace's grave. Dad had a stick and was drawing on a stone they'd laid out in honor of Karma. I peeked over his shoulder to see he had written **'A+'** on it, he looked back at me with a tearful smile.

"We give her an A+." he said.

"She'd love that Pop, she loved her Gramps and Grammie."

We set up a memorial at his house, a collection of the things Karma loved, her food bowl, printed photos, her first birthday tiara and lei, mementos from our road trips, what was left of the toys she destroyed. Her road blanket, her rope monkey. They gave me bereavement at work and I stayed with Dad mostly during the days. Mom and Peter would come by in the evenings and we would remember our girl. There were happy moments we had forgotten, memories that grief brought back to us; experiences Karma had left us like gifts wrapped and tucked behind the tree, waiting to be opened last. The vet called on Friday to let me know her ashes were ready.

Our last night replayed as I followed our path to where I'd left my baby. Pulling the handle on that office door felt like moving ten-thousand pounds. I told them my name and my purpose. The girl working at the desk said she was sorry for my loss, then disappeared into a room and returned with a heavy-looking blue bag. I took it from her and thanked them for everything they had done. The ten-thousand-pound door seemed lighter compared to the weight of that bag.

I carried it back to the Rodeo and sat a moment before I opened it. There was a small oak box inside, it looked like the same tree as Nana's table had been made from. I lifted it out and held it close, it weighed about as much as Karma had when I first got her. The cold polished surface was so far removed from the memory it held. I traced every grain in the wood, every letter of Karma's name burned into its into face.

"What a gift…"

It was all I could think, feel, or say.

I sat her in her seat and she slid up against the seatback and found 'her' spot. I started up the engine and gave her another look. I had no idea how these few pounds in my passenger seat were about to change my life, but she had convinced me to find out. I put us in gear and felt her paw on my heart.

"Let's get you home Sweetheart."

When I was twenty-five, I thought I'd lost everything. I didn't understand what mattered in life, and I'd forgotten how to hope.

And then… I was 41. It was Thanksgiving. I had Mom and Rose hovering over me, both telling me a different thing wrong with the way I was cooking the turkey. Peter and Dad were on the patio talking about crops and livestock, while Maggie zoomed in great circles around the back yard.

I was proud when my TV show worthy turkey came out and my critics jealously conceded that it looked edible. In that moment of victory, I became painfully aware of how uncool my nineteen-year-old self would have thought all this was. With the meal almost ready, Mom went to wrangle Maggie back inside and Rose went to join Peter and Pops on the porch. The sun started setting on the horizon and I started setting the table.

I thought of all the meals that table had seen passed across its oak boards as I laid out the plates and forks, the knives and spoons, how well it had held together all these years, and how the scuffs and scratches and burns were all ornaments of some joy my family had shared or tragedy we'd weathered together. It all told a story. Our story. I thought about all the ideas I'd had about myself and who I was or wanted to be through the years, about how small they all seemed now when weighed against my place in the hearts of these people I loved, and their place in mine.

When the meal was set, we all took our seats. Pops said grace and gave thanks for our time with all the ones we'd loved and lost in our story's telling. A silence filled the room and stirred the familiar smells of the meal we were so blessed to, once again, share. Maggie let out a shrill 'AMEN!' and, after chuckling our own amens, we made our plates and gave her samples as we went.

I looked out over the table, to the empty chair at the other end, where Nana used to sit with her back to the window, looking out over all her young'uns. Through the glass, framed by my family, Nana's backyard stretched out into the dusk, and all my hopes and memories played together at the edge of the light.

A gentle bell from my pocket brought me back into the present. It was a message from Kat:

Happy Thanksgiving!

The words were some of the first I had learned, but stopping then to think about them – to be happy and give thanks – they seemed like the best advice anyone could give on building a good life.

Karma Jean Calloway

June 7, 2007 – October 15, 2022

ABOUT THE AUTHOR

Matthew Calloway is an independent author writing out of Nashville, Tennessee. He was drawn toward fiction's power to create conversations about the nature of the human condition early in life, but it wasn't until 2022 that he found his muse and began work on his first novel, *Good Karma: A Dog's Life.*

Made in United States
Orlando, FL
04 December 2023

40130818R00157